The Untold is...

"...a fast-paced, heart-wrenching story that never loses
speed."—*Library Journal* (starred review)

"...a captivating, epic novel that never loses its heart
to scope."—Patrick deWitt, author of #1 international
bestseller *The Sisters Brothers*

"Astonishing—an utter original. Courtney Collins writes
with brutal honesty, grabbing you by the heart and never
letting go."—Karin Slaughter, *New York Times* bestselling
author of *Cop Town*

"Collins richly evokes a heartbreaking emotional terrain,
setting it against the sparse, brutal landscape of the
Australian Outback."—*Kirkus Reviews*

"This extraordinary novel—propelled by the dark, rich talents of a truly brilliant writer—dazzles, staggers, and amazes."

—Elizabeth Gilbert, *New York Times* bestselling author of *Eat, Pray, Love*

"A captivating, epic novel that never loses its heart to scope, *The Untold* is a surreal saga set in a rugged, unforgiving landscape. Courtney Collins paints a devastating portrait of long-shot love."

—Patrick deWitt, author of #1 international bestseller *The Sisters Brothers* (short-listed for The Man Booker Prize)

"*The Untold* is astonishing—an utter original. Courtney Collins writes with brutal honesty, grabbing you by the heart and never letting go. A shocking, haunting, funny, and ultimately hopeful novel that's also a terrific read."

—Karin Slaughter, *New York Times* bestselling author of *Cop Town*

"Collins's gripping debut novel is based on a legendary wild woman . . . A fast-paced, heart-wrenching story that never loses speed, this extraordinary first novel is not to be missed."

—*Library Journal* (starred review)

"The dead have tales to tell, if only we could hear them . . . Collins richly evokes a heartbreaking emotional terrain, setting it against the sparse, brutal landscape of the Australian Outback."

—*Kirkus Reviews*

"Collins's poetic language and salty dialogue tell the story of a woman whose life is inextricable from the bleak landscape she not only traverses but also inhabits." —*Publishers Weekly*

"This is Magical Realism meets Australia . . . [T]he prose is brutally realistic . . . A fine debut novel." —Historical Novel Society

THE UNTOLD

Courtney Collins

Berkley Books, New York

BERKLEY

An imprint of Penguin Random House LLC
375 Hudson Street, New York, New York 10014

Berkley trade paperback ISBN: 978-0-425-27617-4

The Library of Congress has cataloged the G. P. Putnam's Sons hardcover edition as follows:

Collins, Courtney.
[The Burial]
The untold / Courtney Collins.—First American Edition.
p.   cm.
Previously published by: Sydney : Allen & Unwin 2012, as The Burial.
ISBN 978-0-399-16709-6
1. Hickman, Elizabeth Jessie, b. 1890—Fiction.   2. Australia—History—
20th century—Fiction.   3. Biographical fiction.   I. Title.
PS3603.O4527B87   2014   2013036915
813'.6—dc23

PUBLISHING HISTORY
Allen & Unwin trade paperback edition / September 2012
G. P. Putnam's Sons hardcover edition / June 2014
Berkley trade paperback edition / June 2015

PRINTED IN THE UNITED STATES OF AMERICA

10 9 8 7 6 5 4 3 2 1

Cover art and stepback by Shutterstock.
Cover design by George Long.

Grateful acknowledgment is made to the Random House Group Limited for permission to
reprint lines from "Tonight I Can Write," from *Twenty Love Poems and a Song of Despair* by
Pablo Neruda, published by Vintage Books.

Penguin
Random
House

For my mother, with love

The truth of the heavens is the stars unyoked from their
constellations and traversing it like escaped horses.

—JEAN GIRAUDOUX, *Sodom and Gomorrah*

This is all. In the distance someone is singing. In the distance.
My soul is not satisfied that it has lost her.

—PABLO NERUDA, "Tonight I Can Write"

How could we ever keep love a-burning day after day if it
wasn't that we, and they, surrounded it with magic tricks . . .

—HARRY HOUDINI

This is a work of fiction—inspired by art, music, literature and the landscape, as much as by the life and times of Jessie Hickman herself.

PRELUDE TO DEATH

WHO HASN'T HEARD of Harry Houdini? The Big Bamboozler. The Great Escapologist. The Loneliest Man in the World.

IT IS 1910. Harry Houdini, the World's Wonder, the Only and Original, is up to his armpits in mud. Intractable fingers of sea grass and kelp surge around him. With his eyes open, he can see movement and murky shadows.

He knows that above him twenty thousand people—stevedores, clerks, women in hats—anticipate his death. They line Queens Bridge three deep. Past Flinders Street Station, all the way to Princes Bridge, they crane their necks and jostle for a view. Some have fallen over, tripped on hems and the clerk's pointed shoe, to see him, the World's Wonder, dive into the Yarra, handcuffed and wrapped in chains.

Slapped by sea grass, shrinking from shadows, Houdini brings his wrists to his mouth. With his teeth he pulls out a pin, one from each handcuff. The cuffs fall free and sink farther down.

Houdini grabs at the weeds around him to anchor himself. They are loose and rootless, like slack rope. It is as if the river has no base—just layers and layers of sediment floating upon one another.

He tucks up his short legs and digs his knees into the sludge. His knee scrapes against some rock or reef and he reaches down to follow its seam. He runs his hand over a moss-covered thing, smooth becoming fibrous, until his fingers catch in the familiar loops of a chain. The chain is thick and he follows its links until his hands hit up against a leg iron. And though he is running out of breath and he has yet to free himself from the locks around his neck, his hands seize around the thing within the leg iron. It breaks off. An ankle? A foot? Certainly not rock.

The thing is a thing of limbs.

Houdini gags. He takes in water. The taste is rotten. The thing of limbs is so eaten away by fish that Houdini's grasp has freed it. He is still clutching part of its brittle remains when the larger part of the body floats up and over him. It is the bluntest of shadows.

Houdini beats into the sediment with his legs, stirring up a cloud of silt and other undiscovered things. He swims upwards at an angle, away from the cloud, away from the body, and reaches into his swimsuit for a key. He is just below the surface, veiled by murky water, when he finally frees himself from the locks around his neck. He breaks the surface and raises the locks above his head. Twenty thousand people cheer.

His wet curls conceal his face from the crowd as he turns in the water, searching for the body, the bloated mass. The river reveals nothing but ripples moving unevenly out to sea.

Houdini treads water, waiting for a boat. His chest aches. The rowers move too slowly, their oars striking and slicing the water in a rhythm that does not match the urgency he feels. He coughs and spits as they grow nearer. Finally, one of the rowers reaches down to him while the other balances the boat.

You swallow the river, Mr. Houdini?

Houdini does not answer. He grips the man's arm and hauls himself up and into the boat.

Houdini is silent as the two men row him back to shore. His eyes continue to search the surface of the water but there is no sign of the bloated body and he cannot think of how to explain it or who to tell.

I

*I*f the dirt could speak, whose story would it tell? Would it favor the ones who have knelt upon it, whose fingers have split turning it over with their hands? Those who, in the evening, would collapse weeping and bleeding into it as if the dirt were their mother? Or would it favor those who seek to be far, far from it, like birds screeching tearless through the sky?

This must be the longing of the dirt, for the ones who are suspended in flight.

Down here I have come to know two things: birds fall down and dirt can wait. Eventually, teeth and skin and twists of bone will all be given up to it. And one day those who seek to be high up and far from it will find themselves planted like a gnarly root in its dark, tight soil. Just as I have.

This must be the lesson of the dirt.

MORNING OF MY BIRTH. My mother was digging. Soot-covered and bloody. If you could not see her, you would have surely smelt her in this dark. I was trussed to her in a torn-up sheet. Rain and wind scoured us from both sides, but she went on digging. Her heart was in my ear. I pushed my face into the fan of her ribs and tasted her. She tasted of rust and death.

In the wind, in the squall, I became an encumbrance. She set me on the ground beside her horse. Cold on my back and wet, I could see my breath breathe out. Beside me, her horse was sinking into the mud. I watched him with one eye as he tried to recover his hooves. I knew if he trod on me he would surely flatten my head like a plate.

Morning of my birth, there were no stars in the sky. My mother went on digging. A pile of dirt rose around her until it was just her arms, her shoulders, her hair, sweeping in and out of the dark while her horse coughed and whined above me.

When she finally arched herself out of the hole in the ground she looked like the wrecked figurehead on a ship's bow. Hopeful as I was, I thought we might take off again, although I knew there was no boat or raft to carry us, only Houdini, her spooked horse. And from where we had come, there was no returning.

She stood above me, her hair willowy strips, the rain as heavy as stones. Finally, she stooped to pick me up and I felt her hand beneath my back. She brought me to her chest, kissed my muddied head. Again, I pushed my face into the bony hollow of her chest and breathed my mother in.

MORNING OF MY BIRTH, my mother buried me in a hole that was two feet deep. Strong though she was, she was weak from my birth, and as she dug, the wind filled the hole with leaves and the rain collapsed it with mud so all that was left was a wet and spindly bed.

When the sun inched awkwardly up she lowered me into the grave. Then, lying prone on the earth, she stroked my head and sang to me. I had never, in my short life, heard her sing. She sang to me until the song got caught in her throat. Even as she bawled and spluttered, her open hand covered my body like the warmest blanket.

I had an instinct then to take her song and sing it back to her, and I opened my mouth wide to make a sound, but instead of air there was only fluid and as I gasped I felt my lungs fold in. In that first light of morning my body contorted and I saw my own fingers reaching up to her, desperate things.

She held them and I felt them still and I felt them collapse. And then she said, *Sh, sh, my darling.* And then she slit my throat.

I SHOULD NOT HAVE SEEN the sky turn pink or the day seep in. I should not have seen my mother's pale arms sweep out and heap wet earth upon me or the screeching white birds fan out over her head.

But I did.

S oon it was light enough to see the birds stripping bark with their beaks and the morning was full of the sound of their screeching. My mother stood on my grave, packing down the dirt with her feet. She slid across the smooth river rocks and plunged her arms into the water. Blood, ash and dirt ran down as dark estuaries to her wrists. She turned her hands over in the water until they were clean, until she could see the loops and whorls of her skin magnified.

She said, *Could I cut off my own hands?* And in saying that, she did not sound like my mother at all.

The knife at her belt still had my blood on it. She set the blade at an angle to her wrist but, although she may have doubted it herself, it was not in my mother to cut off her hands or to kill herself. Her hands trembled with her own wish to live and she dropped the knife into the river. She went after it like she was going after a fish but she did not catch it. Instead, she brought up a lump of sand and scrubbed her palms until they were pink and raw. Then she held them up to the sun and said, *Ghost hands,* as the sun seemed to pass straight through them.

My mother raised herself from the edge of the river, sloped over rocks, back to my grave. She sank down on all fours and smoothed over the dirt with her arms and the backs of her hands, erasing her footprints. Back and back she crawled, canceling her tracks and the tracks of her horse, scraping and roughing the earth until she hit water.

She stood knee-deep in the river next to her horse, surveying the ground to be sure she had vanished all traces. To any other observer, they would have appeared as fixed and haunted as two swamped trees.

But my mother was not one to linger.

It was the thought of my father that impelled her then.

What if he's not dead? she said. But there was no one or nothing that could answer back except her own unease, and she pulled herself up onto her horse and turned it into the river. Then they pounded against the current, away from me, away from my grave.

*D*eath is not a simple exit.

When my mother cut my throat she thought she was saving me from some protracted death. But in truth she would have done better to burn me down to ashes with my father than to plant me in the dirt. For it is in the dirt I discovered I have eyes to see and ears to hear, and I can see and hear beyond logical distance and beyond logical time. And with all of these peculiar senses the dirt has brought to life, I wonder if, in our wish to live, my mother and I may not be made of something the same. And then who is there to blame but nature?

When my mother set me down in my grave, the dirt came through like some surrogate mother. It gave me rich feed—food and words and company. It kept me warm and it kept me safe. But still, my mother is my mother. And even with this most generous succor, all that the dirt could muster, I have clung to the simple idea of her returning.

But over time, this simple need for her to return to me, to pick me up and hold me, has sprouted like the most unruly seed and I have found myself tormented and longing for all and everything around her.

Forward and back I have tracked her.

Morning of my birth, my mother tried to put me to sleep in the same way you might put to sleep a pup expelled from its own mother too soon. Any legged creature born two months premature out here did not stand a chance and although my mother suffered to think it, she believed that neither did I.

Beneath the downy fur that covered me, she could see her pup turn blue. And despite her forcing air into my lungs with the explosions of her breath and then the prizing of her thumbs between my ribs as if she might untangle me from death herself, life did not spew forth. I was growing bluer than the sky.

There's a slow rattle in death and she'd heard it before, all kinds of creatures gurgling their way through their final agony. When it sounded from me, she could bear to hear it no more. Death, she thought, was a waiting river, signaling itself in the rising of that sound. She would not wait for its slow claim on me. She was my mother. She would deliver me to it herself.

But right behind that twisted cave of my chest, it was her breath, her thumbs, her love that snagged me and I could not give in to this thing of death. Not yet. Not completely.

THIS IS HOW WE DIFFER, my mother and I:

I do not know death as a river. I know it as a magic hall of mirrors and within it there is a door and the door opens both ways.

y mother pitched her horse against the river. After the rain the current was strong and the water was unknowable. She searched for the split tree she had taken as a marker but through her tiredness the trees all looked the same and then, in narrowing her eyes to see them better, they looked more and more like men than trees, all leaning into the river.

She could not let them find her.

The water was suddenly deep, deeper than she recalled it, and her heart rose inside her as Houdini's hooves scraped and slipped against the river stones. She did not let go of his reins. She urged him on and squeezed her thighs against his sides and tilted her hips forward until at last, with a great surge, his hooves found land.

They had crossed the river.

There was more daylight than my mother wished for, and on this side of the bank their tracks were still visible. The rain had softened them, but they held their form.

She stepped Houdini carefully over them, slow and pained, until the impressions of his hooves forward and back were so close it was impossible to tell which direction they had set off in first.

The forest floor was a webbed mess of fallen branches and

ferns and they galloped over it at full pelt. Their tracks would only matter again when she reached the boundary of Fitz's land.

SHE RODE OUT into Fitz's clearing and angled Houdini along the fence line until they reached the first gate. He was shying and even if she had wanted him to, he would go no farther than the gate.

She swung herself down and unbuckled the saddlebag. Pulling out Fitz's boots, she drained them of water, then walked towards the upper gate barefoot. The long grass was a carpet flattened by rain. She walked past livestock which shifted around her in a silent stupor. From the beginning of the upper gate, there were no trees; Fitz had cleared them all.

There was still smoke rising from the house. Only part of it had tumbled, only part of the roof collapsed. Half looked like it was sliding into a hole while the other half was perfectly intact.

She slid her feet into Fitz's boots, which were heavy—and even heavier wet. The leather against her toe was cracked, a monument to Fitz, to his kicking. Her skin was smarting within them and her bruised hip pained her as she walked. She was thinking that a bruise should not outlast a man. A boot may last, but the bruises he made should vanish with him.

Please be dead, she said. And it was not the first time she had said it.

She pressed her weight into the boots and stepped inside the house. The kettle was still sitting on the stove amid remnants of the chimney.

She moved farther into the remains of the house and felt heat rising into her feet.

Fitz? she yelled.

She pulled up the hatch to the cellar. She could not remember closing it. The boards were creaking and parts of the house were still hissing with flame and damp as she leaned into the mouth of the cellar and searched out the form of him. There was not enough light to see but for small lit patches splattered against broken glass. She held on to the edge of the hatch.

Fitz, you fucker, she called. *Where are you?*

And then she saw him.

Or some of him. An arm. A torso. The strange patterning of burnt skin. A smell rose up of him. The smell of vinegar and onions, just as he had always smelt, and before she could cover her mouth from the stench of it she was vomiting into the cellar.

She was on all fours and the house was sucking the life from her. There was hardly any strength left in her as she wiped her mouth and rolled onto her back. The shock of the morning had finally hit her. Any part of her that was not numb was trembling.

But this is *my* mother.

Lying on her back she pushed with her legs and her feet what mess and rubble she could into the mouth of the cellar. She heard it all crash in around the remains of Fitz and the sound of it consoled her. She did not look back into the cellar but turned herself over and launched herself, unsteadily, to standing. Still wearing Fitz's boots, she staggered from the house and all the way down to the wet grass, collapsing into it.

Fitz was well dead.

She could breathe.

❧

BEYOND THE HOUSE AND FITZ'S FOREST, the mountains spread out north and west. The sight of them, the magnificent stretch of them, was enough to bring my mother to her feet again. She swayed through the paddock towards the gate. Cattle moved quietly around her, looking dim.

When she reached the gate she used it to step up onto Houdini's back. She took his mane and steered his head to face the highest point of the mountains. Then she leaned in close to his ear and said, *My friend, even if I fucking die and rot upon your back, do not stop until we get there.*

orning of my mother's birth was not like my own. She was vital, for one.

Her father, Septimus, had taken her in his arms as soon as Aoife, her mother, had given birth to her in a washtub on the porch.

It was 1894. The night was clear and the sky was full of stars and Septimus watched on like some anxious pop-eyed insect, pressed against the window of his shed. Aoife bellowed and roamed outside as the midwife, Mrs. Peel, tried to steer her back to bed.

But when Aoife caught sight of Septimus at the window, backlit by a fire, his hair sticking on end, she raised her fist to him, and then she slipped. She fell backwards into the washtub and as she did a contraction seized her. When it passed, her legs and neck and arms went limp and she hung over the tub like some overwatered plant.

Septimus watched as Mrs. Peel disappeared and returned again, her arms full of candles and lanterns. She set them all around Aoife's feet, exclaiming, *None of God's creatures shall be born in the dark!* She went about lighting them like a zealot.

Aoife had begun writhing and screaming, *Get it out! Get it out!* And as she writhed a wave of water spilt out of the tub and collected the candles and the lanterns and put them all out.

Mrs. Peel tried to hold down Aoife's legs but they were splitting around her like scissors in the dark. Aoife did not want the child inside of her and she did not want it out. Septimus clutched his heart and cast his eyes skyward. He saw Centaurus there, marking his bow, and the Southern Cross sparkling like some talisman around an upturned neck. He thought at least the beauty of it augured well.

In no time, as this was Aoife's fourth, Septimus heard a trembling wail.

He jumped up, ran to his furnace, thought to put the fire out, changed his mind, caught his shirt on the tin of the door, freed himself, then sprinted across the lawn. He took the child in his arms and Mrs. Peel cut the umbilical cord and then they wrapped my mother in a cloth.

A daughter, said Septimus, leaning down to Aoife to show her.

You take care of her, said Aoife. *I just want to sleep.*

Mrs. Peel helped Aoife inside and Septimus stepped out onto the lawn, my mother curled against his chest. He kissed her damp head and held her above him. She cried and then her little face, still crinkled by the passage of birth, opened up. Septimus saw it as he felt it then: Centaurus drawing his bow among other constellations and firing an arrow straight into his heart. He held my mother and he knew he could never, in all the world, love another trembling creature so much.

YEARS LATER, when my mother asked him what stars he saw on the morning of her birth, he could not describe them. He would only say, *Darling, there were constellations wrapped in the visible sky and the sky below the horizon, and they were all spinning by some force and design. There was a carnival, a parade, on the day you were born and it was spinning around the poles of the universe.*

And although Septimus did know what he saw in the visible sky (an archer, an arrow sent forth) with his own passage through life he had begun to believe more that there was no design in it at all—that the stars themselves were just nebulae visible but indistinct to one another, silhouettes shifting against other luminous matter.

But he did not want to tell that to his daughter.

With her gaze fixed on the mountains, my mother rode all day. Her eyes grew hot and her neck felt too weak to hold her head. Yellow grass streamed endlessly beneath her and she did all she could not to slip sideways into it.

She was losing blood. It soaked into her trousers and the thick skin of her saddle. On the brink of passing out, she lay against the neck of her horse. He was a dam of hot and cold and the feeling was not like riding, it was like sinking and sinking was her fear. She fixed her back like a steel beam and faced the distance.

There was so much distance.

The mountains seemed farther away now than ever and as she tried to focus on the sharp edges of the cliffs where they cut into the sky, they shifted like an unsteady backdrop, one way, then another. The sun was full and bleaching and nothing was solid.

She rode on.

SHE HELD HERSELF UPRIGHT for as long as she could. But even her determination was not enough. Soon she fell against her horse's back and dropped the reins completely.

Houdini, a stallion, a Waler, moved easily from a gallop to a long-striding walk, and the weight of my mother across his back was enough to balance her. He turned east towards the thin arc of river and did not falter from his even step until he reached its bank. Then he shook her from his back and she fell onto the sand.

Hitting the sand she came to. She did not know where she was. She could see Houdini drinking from a part of the river she did not recognize and edged her way to it, put her mouth against it and drank the water until it revived her. She had enough energy then to peel off her sand-encrusted trousers and turn them over to the shallows. Red clouds bloomed out.

My mother was not one to say *oh dear* or *oh my*. She was one to say *fuck*. And often. It was a word she had fine-tuned in prison. Half naked by the river, looking down between her legs, that is what she said: *Fuck, Houdini. I've gone and bled a trail.*

THERE IS NEVER a good day to die. And you'll see my mother is not the quitting kind. But there is courage in blood and she had lost so much of it. She did not have the strength to get back on her horse.

To the north of her were the shifting cliffs and ridges of the mountains. Even if she could have ridden solidly, just to get to the base of the first rise of the mountain range was a whole day's ride. Beside her was the river. If she rolled herself into it and floated down, it would deliver her directly back to where she had come from, the place to which she could not return. Above her was the clearest, bluest sky with no cloud or apparition and it seemed to be sinking down upon her. She covered her face against it.

Fuck, Houdini was the best assessment.

Y ou might like to think of your own mother knitting blankets expanding outwards in all colors while you were in her womb. Or at worst vomiting into buckets. On the eve of my birth, my mother concertinaed my father while I lay inside her. Six foot. Eight inches. She brought him down with the blunt side of an axe.

I was still two moons off by her measure. Already I was large and awkward enough inside her that I was breaking her sleep a couple of times in the night with my knee or my elbow wedged into her bladder.

Eve of my birth I was wide awake, listening to a thrumming sound that I knew was not the sound of her heart. I stretched out and woke her. Hearing the peculiar sound for herself, she lit a lantern and wound up the cloth wick to cast more light. There were two moths attached end to end and they were beating their wings like a fast-rolling drum and making dust on her pillow.

She picked up the moths by the edge of their wings and cupped them both in her palm. She maneuvered a shawl around her shoulders with her spare hand and shifted us all out of bed. Tiptoeing past Fitz's room she saw his door open and his empty bed and she relaxed, walked heavy on her heels.

The moon was just a scrape in the sky and a fog rolled around

the house so she could hardly see beyond it. She stood on the veranda and threw the moths into the air and she was surprised they
did not fly but just dropped to the ground, stuck together, their
wings still beating.

Even with the fog, the air was unseasonably warm with the
turning season and she felt herself being drawn into it. She was barefoot but her feet were hardened and they were as warm in the dirt as
they had been in bed. She ran her hand over the great mound that
was me and she pulled up her nightgown and squatted and pissed.

She preferred squatting on the ground to the humiliation of
carrying the bedpan past Fitz in the morning. When he was not
there, it was her small act of defiance; over the years she had encir-
cled the whole house with her piss, one piss at a time, and she wondered if he would ever pay enough attention to his surrounds to
actually smell it. Imagine what he would do then.

Squatting down in the fog was like squatting in a cloud and the
cloud stretched around her. She realized it was more comfortable
for her to squat than to stand and she rested there for a while, rock-
ing on her haunches. She felt a drop of water on her face and she
wondered if the fog was dissolving but then there were heavier
drops on her arms and her legs and the far-off sound of a storm
breaking.

She pulled down her nightdress and reached the veranda just
before the rain began to pour down. She looked for the moths on
the ground. They were gone or she could not see them.

Her thoughts turned to Fitz. They were not thoughts moti-
vated by concern for him but more the mounting concern she had

for herself and for me inside her. At this hour, every minute that he was not there was a minute he was growing drunker. And no matter how far gone he was, when he returned to the house he may yet have saved a parcel of fury for her especially.

She went inside and rocked from foot to foot by the stove. The light from the fire did not reach the edges of the room and she thought that was a good thing. There was only more dust there and bad feeling. In front of her was the same scene she had looked at for four years or so and it did not please her. It had never pleased her. A roughhewn table with a bench seat on either side and two wooden chairs at each end, and the ominous opening to the cellar, into which Fitz had thrown her too many times to remember. There was nothing else in the room but another fireplace she had seen lit only half a dozen times and two raggedy armchairs.

The armchairs were dead weights and they faced each other. One was narrower than the other and Fitz had designated this one to be hers. It had always looked like a trap to her: so low to the ground, so tall at the sides, and it tilted back in such a way that you could not get out of it easily. The fabric was brown and gold, a pattern of leaves twisting around flowers and flowers twisting around vines, and she could still recall the uneasy feeling of when she first sat in it.

JESSIE HAD just turned twenty-three when, in October 1917, she met Fitz. She was to be his apprentice, breaking in horses for the war and occasionally serving as his domestic. She knew nothing about housekeeping. Every woman vying to leave prison listed housekeeping in her file, regardless of whether she had ever kept a clean house or lived in one. But my mother insisted on listing *horse-breaker* instead of *domestic* because it was the work she knew how to do. Although it was a coveted skill—and one Fitz was looking for—she was discouraged from listing her other significant talent, *horse stealing*, as it was the thing that had landed her in jail in the first place.

As a condition of her release she had to accept an offer of employment and Fitz's offer, as it was outlined to her, seemed to be the best by far. It was the only offer that would not have seen her working for salt in some inner-city terrace, lace upon her head, cleaning up another family's mess or running after another woman's children. She thought she had escaped some terrible fate.

On the day of her release, she waited for Fitz with a warden on the sunny side of the sandstone wall of the prison. She clutched her only bag of belongings. It contained a clean shirt, two pairs of socks, a pair of men's trousers and a dozen soaps that made the canvas bag weigh much more than it otherwise would have. The soaps were the color of candle wax and they were carved into birds and angels and wrapped in tissue, each one a gift from the other women in prison.

She pressed her back against the wall and swapped the bag from arm to arm and the warden said, *Nervous, Jessie?* and she replied, *Never!*

There was heat in the wall and more heat in the day. Her thoughts were on the soaps in her bag, the carved angels and birds, hoping that they would not melt like wax before she could get them safely to wherever she was going.

What is the name of the place? she asked the warden. *And exactly how far is it?*

The Widden Valley, he calls it, said the warden. *It's west or northwest of here. You should ask him along the way. Show your interest, Jessie. It will be a good topic of conversation.*

In the days before her release my mother had begun to look forward to the distinct seasons of life in the country. In her two years in jail, eight seasons had apparently passed, though in her cell it just seemed like one unwavering twilight. The only things that marked a difference for her were the temperature at night, the occasional shifting angle of light on the floor and the number of cockroaches scuttling through her cell.

But when Fitz pulled up in his cart she forgot the promise of the seasons and the soaps in her bag and everything else. He swung down and landed on the footpath in such a way that he seemed larger than both she and the warden combined. He was the most asymmetrical man she had ever seen. And he was red all over: his hands, his face, his hair. She did not know where to look and she was grateful that the warden led him away from her and into the shade to fill out one form or another while she got her bearings by the wall.

She thought to run but resisted it. It would only lead her back to jail. She leaned down and grabbed the laces of her boots in case her feet took off without her. She said to herself, *Don't fuck it up, girl*, and then she fixed her skirt, smoothed her hair and took off her jacket as beads of sweat sprang from every part of her.

When the signing was done, the warden called her over and said, *Jessie, this is Fitzgerald Henry. He is your guardian now and I trust he will be a good employer. He has all the faith of the Crown.*

Jessie shook Fitz's hand. It was rough and damp. Fitz did not say a word. He just nodded his head and then he took her by the elbow and led her to the cart. She glanced at him and then the warden and the warden waved good-bye and that was that. She was not an inmate anymore; she was an employee. So far, it felt the same.

Fitz scooped up the reins and stared straight ahead. She looked at him again. His profile was not flattering. She chided herself. *Have you learned nothing yet? Do not judge a book by its cover. You're not marrying the man; he's your employer. Be grateful. This is your chance to go straight.*

Fitz used a long-handled whip on the gaskins of the horses and they lurched forward and soon he and my mother were careening through the streets of Sydney. Jessie held on to the edge of the cart and peered out.

There was so much to take in.

First, there was a green park which was more like a green knoll where she knew executions had happened and maybe happened still, though now women stood wearing neckties and holding painted signs saying NO! and NO MORE OF OUR SONS! and cars were beeping, more cars than she remembered, cars competing with horses and carts, and then a tram traveling so fast it sprayed shit from the tracks all over the road and in the wake of it she forgot herself and covered her mouth with her skirt until she saw Fitz looking at her legs, and not looking at the road, so she dropped her skirt and covered her mouth with her hand instead and thought what a curious thing modesty was and what a curious thing that she still had any at all. And then she saw women and men meandering along serpentine paths and in a larger park men in army uniform, some alone, some walking hand in hand with their sweethearts around fountains.

And then there were houses in rows. Flat-faced houses, and farther, houses opened up, springing up in spaces with yards and fences between them, and she saw children, *children* playing with hoops and making games with chalk along the roads.

Soon the road widened and they were traveling across a flattened field and it was so hot and dry she thought the horses would expire and she asked Fitz to stop and he said, *Not until we hit the first rise*, and when they hit the first rise he said, *Just a bit farther*. It was the first time they had spoken over the cacophony of noise from the cart and the horses, though she was glad she did not have to answer any questions about life in jail or life before it.

It was pitch-dark before Fitz pulled up at a hotel and watered the horses and checked in at the desk and asked for a drink, but the attendant could not serve him because it was past six o'clock and Fitz said, *Very well*, and asked for one room. My mother had no money to pay for her own and Fitz knew it. She looked at him and he said, *Don't worry, I will sleep on the floor*.

That was her first night beside him.

He snored and she stared at the ornate ceiling and even in the dark she could make out the detail though it was a strain on her eyes and soon she found sleep. Fitz woke her in the morning and said, *Freshen yourself and I will wait for you outside.* But she had nothing to freshen herself with except for a shallow dish of water and a hand towel in the room—not forgetting in her own canvas bag were a dozen soaps, but each one was a thing of hope and she knew they were not just hopes for her but hopes for the women themselves and she would not sacrifice any one of them. So she dampened the small towel and wiped herself down and she could see streaks of dirt appearing with each wipe as if she was wiping away a day, a week, a month in prison. Near the dish of water was a small vase with sprigs of rosemary. She took one and rolled the woody stem between her hands and under her arms and between her legs. The smell released. It smelt clean. She pinned up her hair and when she was done she hung the towel over a chair and pulled the blanket up over the bed. She took her bag. Fitz was waiting outside the door and he led her down to breakfast holding on to her elbow again, the keys to the room jangling from a silver hoop he had attached to his belt, just like a warden.

Over breakfast on the terrace, she turned in the sun, one hundred and eighty degrees, and there was a basket of freshly baked rolls and two kinds of jams and tea in individual pots and she ate as many rolls as were on the table. Fitz asked again for a drink and the waiter said, *I'm sorry, sir, not before eleven o'clock*, and Fitz said, *Very well.*

Fitz drove all day and she offered to drive but he said, *You don't yet know the roads.* That was true but she was not used to being a passenger and her limbs began to shake with the ceaseless motion of it and she regretted eating so many rolls because bread never agreed with her.

But she said nothing more, just held on to the side of the cart and closed her eyes for a while and recalled that the farthest she had traveled in two years was twenty laps at a time around the prison yard.

They reached the beginning of the range and the road wound around and she thought it was an ingenious feat of man to build such a road, but after a while she wondered why he did not think to build a road that went straight over the mountain and came down the other side, rather than one that went in and around bends and cliffs that seemed designed to make a traveler sick and giddy.

Then she saw an eagle as big as a man perched on the edge of a cliff and she was sure it looked over its shoulder and into her eyes before lifting its great expanse of wings and tipping off into a great expanse of sky. She gasped at the sight of it.

That night they did not stop at all and she did not know what Fitz's horses could possibly be made of that they could travel ceaselessly, and by the time the road dipped into a stony track and then dipped into a valley it was midday again and the air was dry and the sun was so bright that she could no longer see anything but fields of yellow, as if the whole place were washed with just one color. Fitz pushed on and on and the fields turned over to the edge of a forest and then everything changed. It was green and dark and damp and when she breathed in the air it felt different in her lungs.

We are close, he said.

Can I walk then? she asked, as she wanted to reclaim something of herself, beginning with the muscles in her legs.

There's no time to waste, he said, and she asked, *Why?* but he did not answer.

When they arrived at his homestead she knew by the way he said *Here it is* that he was proud of it and he had built it himself, but she was not sure what to make of it or what to say, so she said nothing. She just tried to take it all in.

It was a wide house with a wide veranda and there were two chimneys sticking out each end of it. All trees within a hundred yards of it had been cleared and she could see neat fences and holding yards and a shed and a stable.

Come inside, Jessie, Fitz said.

Inside, he poured himself a drink of whiskey and her a mug of water and he said, *Whiskey is not a woman's drink*. But she disagreed.

Then he pointed to the other side of the room and, attempting formality, gestured awkwardly and said, *Be my guest*.

And there it was, the armchair, the trap, and although she saw it that way from the very first sighting, she sat in it anyway. She was thin then from a diet of gruel but still the walled-in sides of the chair did not seem wide enough for her arms, unless she kept her hands in her lap or rested them on the huge panels either side of her, which she did.

Her eyes flicked between her hands and her arms and they had never looked paler. Suddenly, sitting there, she felt ill and her hands did not look like her hands and her arms did not look like her arms and the sight of them haunted her.

Fitz began speaking and she heard him say, *rustling*, and *wife*, and *jail* and still she was trying to take it all in.

Do you understand me? he said.

She shook her head.

It's our agreement, he continued.

She looked up from her arms and straight into his eyes and she said, *No*.

And that was all she said.

The effect of the word on Fitz was immediate. He swelled up like some sideshow spectacle she had seen in the circus. She sat back in the chair and watched a rash spread from his neck to his chin and blossom around his nose so his face became two distinct colors, and then his arms swept down to the floor and wrapped around his chair and he wrestled it towards her.

You will understand, he said.

And then, after the longest ride through the city and over flat fields, around a mountain range and down into a valley, he raised his arm and hit her.

OUT OF ALL THE HOPES that the women in prison had for my mother, carved out in the round faces of angels and birds that flew and some that perched, was one my mother had for herself. Her hope was that her employer was a good man.

But he was not.

Fitz was my father. He was mean and violent and he black-mailed my mother and over time he bruised every inch of her. He had the power of the law over her as her legal guardian and she knew that on the slightest provocation he could cart her back to jail. And if she tried to escape him, he warned her, he would send his men out after her, although she never knew who his men were. Many times she thought jail would be better than life with him, and yet somehow she found freedom in the ways she defied him. Ways he did not know and ways he could never imagine.

Four years on, as she looked over the dusty room and the chairs she hated in the corner, she knew that time was running out. I was on the way and this was no life to be brought into. She would have a child to protect.

She could not have guessed how soon.

It is hard to know what tipped my mother on this particular night to a place so sharp and vengeful. The scrape of moon, the moths, the rain, the memory, all of it fertilized something inside her.

Shifting back and forth on her feet in front of the fire did not ease her discomfort. As the rain pelted down hard on the roof she thought of Fitz falling from his horse and stumbling up the steps and then entering the house as if he owned everything in it, including her, and pressing himself upon her, smelling of whiskey and mud and other women. And as she thought it, anger pulsed within her.

Other nights when she knew he would be drunk she would lock herself in her room, though that would only postpone his rage until the morning.

She scanned the room. Next to the door was a cabinet where he kept his rifles and next to the cabinet was an axe. Fitz kept the key to the cabinet in his pocket so she took the axe instead.

She pressed her back against the side of the cabinet and pushed it with all the strength of her legs. Then she set a chair in its place and sat and listened and waited. She was used to that.

She knew every sound of him. The crashing as he rode through the forest, the thud as he struck through the paddock. All of it: the slapping, groaning, dragging, lurching sounds of him as he approached the house.

And she knew, too, what she had never heard and longed to hear: the sucking sound of the earth as it clung to him and swallowed him up.

*H*alf naked, encrusted in sand, Jessie did not get back on her horse or roll herself into the river. She reached up, pulled a blanket from her saddlebag and wrapped herself in it. She writhed and cursed as pain seized her womb and she bit down on the edges of the blanket to contain it. Then, as three figures moved across the paddock directly towards her, she blacked out.

Had she the strength or consciousness to mount her horse, she would have seen the figures first as shadows thrown across the yellow grass. And eventually she would have made them out: a woman, a man, a dog.

As they approached, she would have seen the man was old, his mouth cragged like barbed wire across his face, his eyes deep sockets like dents in the earth when you kick away a stone. Bits of him were missing. His teeth, a piece of his ear.

The old woman was better put together, though she was surely as old as the old man. Her white hair streamed behind her like spiderwebs and her horse was towing a cart. In the cart was a dead lamb.

The old woman and the old man were following the dog.

The dog was a yellow stripe with yellow eyes, and he zigzagged out in front of them. He vanished in the long grass of the paddock and the old woman and the old man kept track of him by the splitting and crackling of the grass where he went. They were both eager and charged by the find of the lamb and they were confident the dog would sniff out any warm-blooded creature within a mile of them.

THE DOG WAS a hunting dog and the old man had found him a year or so before, tied up to a tree. He had heard the dog barking in the valley as clearly as if the dog had been barking in an amphitheater. He followed the sound until he finally saw the dog in the distance, just a streak of a thing leaping up and down, barking a frenzy. As the old man rode in closer, the dog launched himself so far the rope around his neck snapped him back and his feet went skidding out from under him.

The old man dismounted his horse and took a hessian sack out of his saddlebag. He walked slowly towards the dog and as he did the dog shook himself. His skin flapped around his bony legs like a curtain. He goaded the dog, *Come on, you wretch, smell that!* and pushed the sack out in front of him. It was the same sack he used for rabbits and their scent was all over it. The dog latched on to it as quickly as anything. The old man wrapped the dog's rope around his muzzle and sank the bag right over him.

The dog thrashed in the old man's arms and the feeling of the dog enlivened him. Walking around the tree, the old man could see the dog had worn a circular track and there were bones and the remains of the dog's past owner scattered around it.

The old man laughed then as he understood the dog to be a prize. Within the dog's thrashing body was all that was fading in the old man. Wretched though the dog appeared, here was a creature whose senses were still primed, a creature so intent on life he ate his owner to survive.

WEAVING THROUGH the yellow grass the dog sniffed out my mother. He had caught the scent of her as surely as if she had dragged her bloodied trousers with a stick for a mile behind her.

He tore across the sand and plunged his snout into her neck. She was in and out of consciousness still but she woke to it, to see teeth and saliva. The dog barked into her ear and her head rang with voices and the sound of other dogs barking. My mother was not a religious woman. She did not believe in heaven and she did not believe in hell, but at that moment she thought she had been wrong after all and that hell, finally, was the place she had found herself. The dog was in a fit, savaging the blanket to get to the source of her blood, and she thought, *This is what happens in hell. Dogs disembowel you.*

But what my mother took as other dogs of hell moving in on her was the old man and the old woman swinging down from their horses and grunting and croaking as they scrambled down the bank and then the sound of the old man lifting the yellow dog with his boot and the dog's mournful howling.

Soon their pale faces hovered over her. And with their strange eyes and mess of silvery hair my mother took them to be harbingers of death, as surely as she knew a frost was a harbinger of winter.

You're late, she said. Because in truth she believed that death had already come to her.

But she was not dead nor were they harbingers of death. They were old and they were human and they began quarreling about what to do with her.

My mother had been set up. It began years before my birth. She was just five months out of prison. She was still in the land of hope then, and she hoped directly to the leaf and the dirt as much as to the sky and the mountain that things would get better. She buried herself in her work and tried to prove herself to Fitz through her efficiency and her talent for breaking in horses. But the only acknowledgment he had given her was a walloping when he found her petting the horses in the evening when she should have been preparing his dinner.

She hated him already and it was only the beginning of her first autumn there.

There was some reprieve. Mostly, Fitz disappeared during the day and returned to the house only just before sunset. That left her alone to do her work and enjoy the peace and challenge of the horses. Day by working day she could feel her balance and her strength returning. But with the turning of the season, she noticed the nights were coming sooner. And although there was a time she thought she would welcome every change of nature, she knew that soon there would be much less daylight to get things done and much less time to be free of him. She feared what a winter alone with him would bring.

THE NIGHT OF THE SETUP, it was just on dusk, the time she expected him. The sun was her clock and it had all but sunk and there was no sign of Fitz—or, rather, no ranging sound of him.

She set the table as he had instructed her to do, with the forks lined up against the knife and the spoon and a napkin folded in a triangle. She wrapped the plates in a tea towel and put them on the stove top to warm. She sampled the stew. She waited, warding off an uneasy feeling.

It was fully dark when she heard a cavalcade of horses and it was not the sound she expected to hear or the sound she was used to. She pulled at the wooden door of the gun cabinet and was thankful Fitz had forgotten to lock it. He usually always locked it and he usually always kept his guns loaded. She grabbed a rifle, crouched down and peered through the front window.

There were two men approaching the house and neither of them was Fitz. Beyond them she couldn't quite see but she knew she was hearing the muster of at least half a dozen horses, and if they were being mustered there must be more men.

There was a banging on the door.

Fitz? yelled one of them.

Jessie crawled beneath the window and stood behind the door. She yelled back, *What?* It was her best impression of Fitz.

We've got the horses, said the voice on the other side of the door.

Fitz had not told her of any delivery. But he never told her of anything. She concealed the rifle on one side of her and opened the door.

Sorry, ma'am, said one of them, surprised to see her. *Is Fitz in?*

Both men looked like droving types. Tall and lean. They kept their hats on.

He'll be back soon, said Jessie. *Do you have business with him?*

We do, but we won't stick around if he's not in.

Was he expecting you?

Yes, ma'am. Told us to deliver the horses tonight.

They'll need to go into the holding yard, said Jessie.

And they need rebranding quick smart, said one of the men.

I'll get to them in the morning, said Jessie.

You might want to get to 'em sooner.

They stolen? she asked.

I'm just saying, ma'am. You might want to rebrand 'em tonight, before dawn.

༼ ༽

BY THE TIME Fitz arrived back at the homestead the next day, Jessie had rebranded the stolen horses and she had chosen one for herself, the dapple-gray Waler she named Houdini. She was riding him in the paddock when she heard a gunshot. The horse reared up but she was able to calm him. She turned to see Fitz riding out of the forest. Even from far off she could tell he was drunk by the way he was swaying back and forth in his saddle.

He was riding towards her and he was aiming his gun. She dismounted Houdini and stood in front of him.

You aiming that gun at me?

{ 43 }

You've got an imagination, he said, dropping the gun to his side. *I see you've been busy.*

I've been branding your horses.

Well done, he said. *Come up to the house. I've a present for you.*

At the house, Fitz pushed a brown package across the table and Jessie unwrapped it. Inside was a long white cotton dress with a hem of embroidered roses.

Why would I want a dress? she asked. *I'm perfectly at home in my trousers.*

Go and put it on, Fitz said.

She did not. Instead, she busied herself lighting the fire.

Fitz sat down and put his feet up on the table. *You're looking at a year for each horse.*

I haven't stolen any horses, said Jessie.

Unless there's something wrong with my eyes, half a dozen horses have appeared in the holding yard.

The horses were delivered for you.

But it was you who took delivery of them. And I suspect I could track down the owners.

She knew what was coming. All of these months he had been biding his time, unable to accept no as an answer.

Jessie, you have two options that I can see.

And what are they?

I can take you back to the same jail I collected you from.

Or?

You can marry me.

MY MOTHER CHOSE but it was a false choice. On the same day that Fitz had swayed out from the forest he doubled her back into it. He was dressed in a blue suit and his hair was slicked back and she wore the long white dress. They rode fast beneath low-hanging branches and when Fitz yelled, *Duck!* she did and then she did not. She held up her arms and the branch hooked her but only for a second before she fell to the ground and when she stood up he slapped her.

That afternoon, the justice of the peace—the postmaster—who married them made a note in his book that the bell sleeves on the bride were ripped in places and speckled with blood. No family or friends were present. The bride appeared unsettled but in the end the postmaster took the groom's money and a photo and he did not ask any questions other than *Do you take this man?* and *Do you take this woman?* And they both said, *Yes,* and then they both signed.

*B*eside the river my mother blacked out again. The old man rolled a cigarette while the old woman dropped to her knees and began unwrapping the blanket to determine the source of my mother's bleeding.

The old woman was muttering, *I will save you, I will save you,* which irritated the old man exceedingly.

Woman! he screamed finally. *She's too far gone. And if she lives she'll surely be trouble.*

I will not leave her, said the old woman, and she was calm and defiant and she kept about what she was doing.

She's just another mouth for me to feed, said the old man. He sat down on the sand and his dog sat down beside him.

The old woman stood up and raised a crooked finger to the old man. *All of these years in this miserable place I have prayed for the company of someone other than you and here she is. I am taking her.*

The old woman shuffled over to the river to wet her handkerchief to clean up my mother.

She's of no value, said the old man, sucking in his breath. Then he lit his cigarette and poked the air with it, pronouncing, *Woman, nothing is of value in this world if it does not fight.*

The old woman was not listening. She was slightly deaf anyway and distracted by my mother's trousers, which were still billowing and bloody in the shallows of the river. She reached after them with a stick.

While the old woman's back was turned, the old man stooped over my mother to examine her. Her brow was heavy and her jaw was sharp and he did not like the look of her. Her dark hair fanned out in a tangle around her and for all he knew she could be some runaway, some murderer—which, in fact, she was.

He crouched right over her and blew smoke into her face.

My mother opened her eyes and saw the old man and she did not know what he was but she knew he was danger. She took a gurgling breath and she coughed up something from the depths of her. And then she spat it dead center between the old man's eyes.

The old man went hurtling back, falling onto his dog, who was whimpering and howling. The old man hooked his arm around the dog's neck and said, *Don't worry your mongrel head. If she does not die here, I will kill her.*

*M*orning of my birth, the sounds of Fitz were in-distinguishable against the rain. He was already scraping his boots on the steps before my mother realized he was there.

She had grown tired in her waiting, but on hearing him she was suddenly awake, suddenly standing on her chair, all seven months pregnant of her, steadying herself against the wall as Fitz wrestled with the handle of the door.

He flung the door open. It hit the edge of the chair and she could see him pitching back and forth and then there was no time for hesitating.

Her anger surged within her and pulsed through the wooden handle of the axe, and as Fitz lurched forward she threw the axe across his back and he was so drunk he fell down immediately. He roared and she leapt down from the chair before he could get up and she swung the axe down again across his back and she did not stop swinging till she was certain that he could not walk or lift himself up from the ground ever again.

NOT *EVERY* DAY is a good day to be born and whatever bright stars were concealed by clouds that morning and whatever their angle, they did not bode well for me. As my mother took the axe to my father a wave rose inside of her and pushed me up and turned me over till I felt sick and deaf to everything. Till I grew cold. When I could not hear her heartbeat I panicked. I kicked and twisted and dug my heels in where I could and then I felt her drop to her knees and, worse, I felt the wild sea inside her spill out.

My birth, though months too soon, was not an agony. I put all of my weight onto my head and bore down. My mother moved around me like a snake sliding out of old skin. And then I thought I heard bells ringing and I fell into the bells of her hands and that was my birth.

I opened my eyes and thought: *Is this life?*

I saw my poor mother gasp at the sight of me. There was just enough light to make me out and I felt her mouth around my mouth and her breathing into me and then spitting out all of that wild sea I had drunk in. She shook me from side to side and covered my mouth with her mouth again. And then she grabbed me by the feet and swung me around and smacked my arse, and I thought, *Fuck, Houdini! What life is this?*

I heard my mother sobbing. She held me in her arms for a while and then she carried me over to my father's view. I looked into his dark eyes and I saw them grow wide and I heard a crack as his head hit the floor.

I saw my reflection in his eyes. Covered in fur, unlovely, I do believe it was the sight of me that finally killed him.

MY MOTHER TRIED to feed me milk from her breast but no milk would come. She put hot washcloths over her chest and she tried to feed me again. But I could not breathe and I could not feed, so she bathed me in warm water while my father grew cold at her feet. And then she bundled me up in a sheet and tied me to her before she smashed the gun cabinet with the axe and took out a rifle. She dragged Fitz to the opening of the cellar and then, with her feet, she rolled him in. She poured kerosene into the mouth of it and into every dark corner of the house. She threw a match into the cellar and then match after match until it threw back flames. With what was left of the kerosene she drenched those armchairs and set them ablaze.

The flames leapt up and the sound was like Fitz on a tirade. But we were safe and already outside. I clung to her as she saddled her horse, packed a blanket, a gun, a knife.

The rain was upon us. We could hardly see where we were going. We rode anyway.

II

t best, if the weather held, Jack Brown was a day's ride from Fitz's place.

He had been riding since dawn. Finally, just as the sun was setting, he had in his bleary sights those rocks as perfect as squares which signaled to him the end of the northern range and the beginning of the valley. He rode on and the land leveled out and the rocks overlapped like scales on some creature's back. Trees fell away on either side, as if it had cleared a path to find its rest, its tail winding down into the valley, disappearing into darkness.

Jack Brown rode on through the night. The sky gave enough light so he could just make out the ground, which was a litter of branches, and he stepped his horse over them and moved into clearings where he could.

He was desperate to get to her.

He had made the delivery, wound through the gorges he had come to know so well, three weeks' riding with stock in tow, one week back without. He had not lost one sturdy cow. His job was done. Fitz should be happy with that.

He had rehearsed it so many times on so many rides—what it would be to finally stand up to Fitz, to ask to be paid, to quit. Jessie had warned him that with Fitz there could be no reasoning, that the only way out was to escape, or he would most certainly have them both thrown in jail. They must wait is what she had said. But his question now was his question then: *Wait for what?*

In his three years in the valley, Jack Brown had herded and branded stolen cattle for Fitz, unknowingly and then knowingly. Until Fitz discovered her pregnancy, Jessie was there for every ride and for every heist. Fitz had kept his hands clean of it all and threatened to incriminate them both if ever their loyalty wavered.

But there was no loyalty because there was no freedom. There was only an oppressive bind. Fitz held on to a whole stable of horses as evidence of their crimes. Jack Brown knew that a black man had no more power than a convict woman, maybe less, and they could never plead a case of blackmail or rely on white man's justice. But as much as he did not want to be imprisoned or see Jessie imprisoned again, he also did not want to be Fitz's captive or his fugitive. He held out for the chance to reason with him, man to man.

Over the long ride, when Jack Brown played it in his head, he did see a man. It was the man of himself, riding through Fitz's forest, having delivered a hundred head of cattle; a man fully possessed of his own power, his own worth. He would arrive at Fitz's homestead, walk surely up the steps, remove his hat. He would be tall at the door and stand strong. He would shake Fitz's hand and they would bargain for his freedom and for Jessie's.

But he did not know what to bargain with. And as often as he played it, it never came to him what to say or how to say it. He only hoped that the man of himself, in the moment of his facing Fitz, would truly know his worth and the right words would flood his tongue, just as prayers come to desperate men when they need them.

⁊⸈

AS HE RODE into the valley a storm rolled down from the northern range and clouds turned over themselves like rabbits chasing their own tails. Jack Brown took in the vastness of it and saw that there were two distinct skies, one that was churning and one that was not. He was glad to be on this side of it.

He had covered a lot of ground in good time and when he finally reached Fitz's forest the sun was going down again, and though his body felt spent, his mind was clear. He was certain of what he had to do next.

He rode into the thick of the forest. The last of the sunlight moved around him in giddy, skipping lots until it was gone completely. The darkness of the forest did not bother him. He had ridden through it so many times that he could have made his way with his eyes closed, just by the smell of it and the weight and drift of air on his skin.

Soon he heard the sound of a creature moving near him. In itself that was not unusual, but the creature sounded like a horse and he knew that no horses roamed loose in Fitz's forest because nothing of value roamed free under Fitz's reign.

Jack Brown rode through the undergrowth, ducking to avoid the low branches. He could hear the creature tearing up grass and he was almost upon it when he saw its silhouette. The horse reared up. He swung down from the saddle and moved in closer, calming the horse with his voice. When it had quieted, he felt for markings on its hind quarter. It was one of Fitz's. He tossed a rope around its neck and once it was secured the horse made no protest. He mounted his own horse again and led the stray out of the clearing and back through the undergrowth.

He rode on.

Before he reached the edge of the forest, Jack Brown came across another two of Fitz's branded horses. There was barely enough length in the rope but he looped a neck hold for each of them and secured them. He moved along slowly so there was a stepping length between the horses. They should not be in the forest. He could think of no good reason. He was not heartened by finding them or by the way they stepped like prisoners behind him.

WHEN HE REACHED the first gate of Fitz's paddock Jack Brown thought to lead the horses into the holding yard. The second gate was already open. A few livestock sauntered within the paddock. He rode through the second gate. Remaining on his horse, he closed the gate behind him and let the other horses loose. They scattered in different directions. He kicked his own horse into a gallop and rode fast up the rise.

He was sure his eyes were failing him when he saw the house and he stood up in the stirrups for a better view. As he could make it out, part of the roof was caved in and the other side buckled at strange angles. He pulled up his horse and turned on it, one way then another, then he pushed on towards the house.

His concern about what to say to Fitz and how to say it was taken over by thoughts of my mother. *Where is she? Is she safe?*

Jack Brown slid from his horse while it was still moving, and stepped onto the veranda. His eyes were not deceiving him.

Jessie! he called, and then, *Fitz!*

He walked through the door that was already open.

Jessie! he yelled, and kept on yelling. But nobody answered.

He walked through the house. His boots crashed against all kinds of things. When he thought he heard some movement, he stopped dead. But then he realized it was the sound of his own moving chaos.

❧

THAT NIGHT HE CAMPED in the stable. When he checked the horses he saw that Houdini's stall was empty. He lay down to sleep but despite his exhaustion he hardly slept at all. There were so many possibilities racing through his head, thoughts turning over thoughts. *Was she dead? Was she gone?*

He was not on the clear side of the sky at all.

He fell into a tense spell of sleep just before sunrise and when he woke he thought he heard Fitz's voice shouting orders to him from the veranda. He sprang from his bed of hay, brushed himself down and ran up to the house like he would have any other morning. But where every other morning something cringed inside him at the sight of Fitz, now he cringed at the sight of the house and the sight of him gone.

In the light of the morning Jack Brown could see that most of

Fitz's horses and cattle were missing and those that remained were subdued and heavy in the legs, tottering aimlessly as if they had all eaten some nullifying weed.

The house, too, looked like a sick thing with its cowering head. Around its smashed windows and open door was charred wood and the residue of flames spiraled out to its edges.

Inside was the same mess and tangle Jack Brown had traced the night before. But by daylight he could see there were footprints and the footprints were not his own. They were Fitz's. He was sure of it. They led in towards the cellar and they led back outside.

Jack Brown pulled furniture and other charred things from the opening of the cellar and lowered himself down. He pressed his hands and feet against the sandstone walls and when his feet reached something solid he planted himself on it. He lit a match. The floor was a soup of mud and shards of glass and piles of salt. Against a wall was a shelf lined with cracked jars and sacks piled up, some of them still whole, but most of them split right open.

His eyes adjusted, Jack Brown surveyed the cellar, turning in the small space. He balanced on bricks until he realized that the bricks were balancing on some other thing. He kicked away the rubble and he saw what he did not want to see. It was Fitz—or what remained of him. Jack Brown could make out his grimy torso, his arm and the buckle of his belt glinting in the dark.

He pressed both hands against the wall. He thought: *It should not have come to this. Did he kill Jessie first and then kill himself? Is her body here as well?*

And then: *I am done for. A black man standing over the remains of his white boss. If I thought justice would not serve me then, I know it will not serve me now.*

Jack Brown pulled a sack from the shelf and tore it open. He poured out its contents; he could not tell if it was sugar or salt but he was not about to taste it. He thought, *Salt would preserve him best—but why would I want to preserve him at all?*

And just like the old man had done with the dog, Jack Brown opened the sack right up and filled it with his find. But unlike the old man, Jack Brown did not regard Fitz's body as any kind of prize. Fitz was dead. There was no life left in him and there was nothing that Jack Brown could do to reverse it. He dragged the sack up and out of the cellar.

He was still not certain that Jessie was not in the cellar too, so he lowered himself back down and lit matches and moved things around until no part of the cellar was unturned. Only then was he certain. She was not there.

But where was she?

He followed the tracks of Fitz's boots, first to the veranda and then out through the mud to the edge of the grass. Jack Brown knew Fitz's prints, the size and weight of them in the dirt, and he knew the length and unevenness of his stride. He pressed his fingers into the indentations in the ground and he knew they were not made by Fitz. He guessed it. Jessie had worn Fitz's boots. She had killed him and she was gone.

Was this what he was to wait for after all?

He mounted his horse with the grim haul and headed back towards the forest.

*T*he old woman got her way. She picked up my mother by the hands; still cursing her, the old man picked up my mother by the feet and they loaded her into the cart next to the dead lamb.

It was a slow ride back to the base of the mountains. Leading on his own horse, the old man pulled Houdini along, tight-reined, punishing him with a kick to his flanks every time he turned towards Jessie. The old woman rode unevenly behind them.

When my mother woke it was dark. She arched her neck back to see the old woman, her hair swinging from side to side as she rode, her horse pulling the weight of the cart, jolting as they moved up the slope.

The moon was still thin but the stars were bright and lit the trees enough to make shadows. As the cart moved through the forest, the shadows passed over it. The cart canted more and more with the slope and my mother could see the path they had already traveled. On that path she could see herself standing, and then she could see that self growing distant. She turned away from it. She trained her eyes between the wooden slats of the cart and out into the forest, but there again she saw herself, or versions of herself, like children running between trees.

∝‿∾

INTO THE WOODS: the game they played when the moon was full and later, when they had their courage, when the moon was dark. Their house was not far, but not visible, so the forest was all and their own.

Jessie was a child then, too tall for her age, too wild and too tall, trying to find her father, her sister, her brothers, all of them yelling to her, *I'm here, I'm here*, then running between the trees. She crouched low, held on to a flashlight, a new thing of light, and turned it sharply in the dark.

I'm here! A body would leap and weave between the trees.

I'm here!

She would run until she felt her heart exploding.

One night she ran so far that the sounds of them were lost to her and she felt they were gone, and not just gone but gone forever, and the feeling was real and she could not hold back her sobbing.

Where are you?

Through her tears the trees were doubling and shifting like legged creatures.

Where are you? Is that you?

Her father stepped out from behind a tree in the distance.

Jessie! he yelled. *I'm here.*

She ran to him.

You're crying, my love.

I thought I'd lost you. She grabbed hold of his arm and wiped her eyes with his sleeve.

Darling, he said, *you can't lose me.*

Her father took her hand and they walked along the broken path until her two brothers and her sister leapt out and said, *We're here!* Then they all walked together, all holding hands, taking turns with the flashlight, their feet never touching the circle of light that was always ahead.

y mother did not know what world she was in. She was in and out of feverish dreams and of course I tried to reach her. I could not reach out with hands or feet, so I bawled out, *Mother, there is life! Don't die. Not yet!* And I willed us as one and I imagined it was us riding together hell-bent up the mountain, disappearing into its shadows. All was dark there and we were protected. But even in my dreaming, where I wanted my mother to feel peace, I could only feel her terror—and soon I realized that this was not my dream at all.

My mother was dreaming me back.

In her dream, we were not escaping together into the mountains. She had us in the old woman's cart, but it was not a horse towing us, it was the old woman herself. The cart was bouncing over rocks and my mother stuffed me inside her shirt and opened the latch with her toes and slid out of the cart and then she sprinted into the dark. When she heard the old woman holler, she dropped to the ground and we rolled and we rolled until we hit a log. She crawled into it and she held me tight and told me to be as quiet as I could.

She's gone! the old woman screeched, and then the sound of the cart rattled through the forest with the sound of the dog tearing through.

The dog found us in no time and circled the log. He pushed his snout right in and we could see his teeth and we shrank back and back but there was nowhere to go. The old man grabbed my mother's hair and pulled us out.

You can't escape smelling like that, he said.

MY MOTHER'S DREAMS did not end there. She was scrambling barefoot up the mountain, pursued not by anything that she could name but by looming shapes that moved steadily and changed direction only when she turned to face them.

When she woke, she was lying in a room she did not recognize with a heap of knitted blankets piled upon her. She was sweating all over. The sheets were damp and she kicked them from her and when she raised her hands to rub her eyes, she saw her nails had been clipped and shaped and cleaned. There was a silver bracelet around her wrist. She tried to pull it off but it was too small for her hand and it pushed up against her bone and scraped her skin. It felt to her like a handcuff.

She sat up and pressed her feet into the floor and her head felt light and the floor looked to be a long way away. She examined her feet. Her toenails had been clipped too and she had never seen her feet so clean.

She was dressed in a nightgown. Lace fringed her neck and scratched her skin. It was cold out of bed. There was no window in the room but a draft streamed up between the floorboards. A dog barked outside and she could hear the voice of an old man. She remembered the barking and the voice and then the face of the old man leaning over her.

She searched the room for her clothes but could not find them. Aside from under the bed there was nowhere to look. There was nothing in the room except the bed, a kerosene lamp and a chair. She wrapped herself in one of the knitted blankets and opened the door.

SHE WAS STANDING in a sunlit kitchen. The wall facing her was made entirely of window frames, jigsawed together. They rattled in the wind. Outside, a stick flew through the air and the dog ran after it. She could see a cleared yard; from the rise of it and the way it was littered with bush rock she guessed she was very near the base of the mountains.

The dog reappeared with the stick in his mouth and the old man walked into view. My mother's first instinct was to hide from him so she crouched beneath the window. But she realized immediately that hiding was a foolish thing because here she was, already in his house, dressed in his wife's nightgown, which meant she had already been found. She stood up slowly and hoped he had not seen her attempt to hide. She tugged the blanket around her shoulders and tied it in a knot at the small of her back so it looked like a shawl.

She stood tall, hoping her fear would not reveal itself to the man or the dog.

⁓

THE OLD MAN did see her. Ducking down and rising up and then standing at the window. He took the stick from the dog and pointed it and walked towards her. *Look here*, he said, tapping the stick on the glass. *She's risen from the dead.*

His voice warbled in her ear and the sound of it chilled her.

She was standing there, her arms folded across her chest, wondering what to do next, when the old woman burst through the door.

Oh, child!

The old woman pushed her back against the door to shut it, and held on to her hair which was twining around her.

Where are my clothes? said my mother.

With that old blanket around you, you looked like a harpy at the window. The old woman chuckled. *Only, harpies belong outside.*

My mother was not amused. *Where are my trousers, my shirt, my boots?*

You weren't wearing no boots, child, said the old woman. *Not when we found you. And you'd made a mess of your clothes. You'd lost your pants and that shirt you had on was no better than a rag.*

Where is it? said my mother. *I'll wear it anyway.*

Enough of that, said the old woman. *We'll deck you out with new kit, no problems there. But first things first. Hungry is surely what you are. We'll give you a feed and get some flesh back on those bones of yours.*

My mother was hungry. She did not know what to make of the old woman but her hunger was sure.

What is there to eat around here?

The old woman patted her on the shoulder and moved towards the stove. She lifted the lid on a pot which gave way to the thick smell of gravied meat. It made my mother's mouth water and she felt faint. She held on to a chair.

The old woman buzzed around the kitchen, setting the table, and then she said, *Sit down, dear. That's what guests are supposed to do.*

Is that what I am? said my mother, and she sat down. She didn't have the energy to pursue the question *What am I doing here?*

The old woman poked at the coals within the stove and then tasted the contents of the pot with her finger. *Ooh yes,* she said. *That friend of yours does taste good.*

My mother reared up from the table and knocked back her chair.

You fucking killed Houdini? she spluttered.

The old woman spun around. She was holding a spoon out in front of her.

I'll not have your foul language here. I've heard enough of your mouth in your fever. And what are you talking about now? Who's Houdini?

My horse! said my mother. *Have you butchered my horse for your dinner?*

Oh, child, said the old woman, turning back to the pot. *It's the lamb I'm talking about, that lamb in the back of the cart—the one you were clinging on to like it was your own beloved.*

My mother sat down again, feeling nauseous at the thought.

And I don't know if it's no Houdini, but we found a horse loitering by you on the bank of the river.

Where is he?

He's in the stable. So everything is as it should be, dear. Every single thing on earth is in its place.

The old woman ladled out the contents of the pot.

You'll take me to him?

Only after you eat, said the old woman. She set a bowl in front of my mother. The stew was dark and glossy with fat and hunks of lamb.

How long have I been here? asked my mother.

You spent a good couple of days in a fever, cussing at the ceiling, and a couple more just sleeping it off. I don't know, dear—almost a week.

What did I say in my fever?

Oh, a whole lot of gibberish and nonsense. You copped the old man a spit in the eye and a punch in the chops, though, so who knows if you were actually sleeping? The old woman laughed again.

I'm sorry for that, said my mother and she began to eat heartily.

No mind, said the old woman. *We all have our ways.*

My mother put her head down and ate so close to the bowl she could have scalded her chin. The stew was salty and good and she did not lift her eyes until the bowl was empty. The old woman did not eat but sat opposite, watching her intently.

My mother noticed her staring only when she had finished eating.

Not hungry? she asked.

The old woman reached across the table and covered my mother's hand with her own. *Only for your company, dear*, she said. She lifted her eyes skyward. *You see, God has finally answered my prayers.*

My mother snatched back her hand.

What is this? said my mother, raising her wrist with the bracelet.

It's a gift, said the old woman.

I don't want it.

Why?

It hurts my hand.

The old woman snapped the bracelet open and pulled it off my mother's wrist.

I thought you would appreciate it.

I've got no interest in such things.

You know how to hurt an old woman's feelings.

The old woman's presence began to oppress my mother.

I'm not feeling well, she said. *Can you take me to Houdini? And then I should go back to bed.*

You can rest all you need to, dear, said the old woman. *And your horse is right there. But first you must bathe.*

Soap and water irritate me, said my mother and she was not lying. It was one of her defenses against Fitz, to bathe not very often or not at all.

They may well, dear. But this is my house and there are certain rules and you must wash that fever from you or else catch it from yourself again and your insides turn septic.

All right, I will bathe, said my mother, *but first I need to see my horse*.

The old woman tut-tutted but she cleared Jessie's plate, then led her outside.

~⁓~

HOUDINI WAS IN A STABLE that had been cobbled together out of found things but it had a roof and a dirt floor and there was hay scattered within it. There was feed and fresh water. Jessie did not understand the motives of the old man or the old woman but she was glad that at least they knew how to take care of creatures.

And there he was, Houdini, seventeen hands high, her dapple-gray stallion, bowing his head over the stable gate when she walked in. At the sight of him, she felt her heart tear. Houdini, more than anyone or anything, was her witness to it all.

Houdini scooped her chin with the bridge of his nose and my mother touched her nose to his. She found a brush inside the stable and brushed him down—though she only managed to brush one flank and a hindquarter before all of her energy was gone.

From outside the stable, the old man kept an eye on her while he cleaned and polished a saddle. Jessie recognized it to be hers. There were bloodstains on the seat and she was embarrassed by the very sight of it.

Where is she? she asked.

The old man gestured to a tin shed near the far side of the yard. *Preparing your ablutions*.

Jessie walked towards the tin shed, feeling the old man's eyes on her all the way.

⁌⁍

THE BATHHOUSE WAS BUILT around a water tank. There were three walls with a roof but one side of it was completely exposed to the weather.

Get undressed, dear, said the old woman.

My mother looked towards the opening.

Don't worry, dear. He won't bother you. I'll make sure of that.

The old woman disappeared. My mother peered around the tin wall, then pulled the nightgown up and over her head. It felt good to be out of it. She stepped into the tub. The water was warm and came to just above her ankles.

The old woman returned with pots of hot water and poured them into the bath.

Go on, she said. *Keep the tap running and lie down in it while it's warm.* She perched on the edge of the bath while my mother sat down in the water and stretched her legs out.

The old woman wrapped a cloth around a brick of soap and began to rub my mother's back.

I'll do that, said my mother. *I do know how to wash myself.*

I thought you said you didn't.

I'll do it when you are gone.

The old woman's eyes narrowed and she scanned my mother's body.

Have you never seen a naked woman before? said my mother.

And then a look came over the old woman and her forehead flattened, as if she was unveiling herself at last.

Child, I know it's not long ago you gave birth. You are all bones except out in front.

My mother shook out the brick of soap and covered herself with the cloth. *You don't know anything about me.*

I know your name is Jessie, said the old woman. *It was written on your shirt, as if you'd come from a prison or some dormitory. Is that where you have come from?*

My mother did not answer.

And there is no hiding that you were not long ago with child. Your milk is all over the bedsheets and it is seeping from your nipples now.

Jessie brought her knees up to her chest and raised her eyes to the top of the water tank.

Where is it? said the old woman.

What?

The child.

Buried.

Was it stillborn?

No. It was born live. But too soon.

Oh, child.

I'm not a child.

I know.

The old woman's chin began to tremble and tears filled her eyes. She started to sob.

Please stop, said Jessie. She could hardly breathe in the old woman's presence.

The old woman wiped her face with her skirt.

Can you leave me alone?

The old woman left the bathhouse without protest. Jessie could hear her sobbing as she walked around the water tank. And then she was gone.

My mother leaned back against the end of the bath and watched her body rising and falling with her breathing. She held her breath for a long time and wondered how long it would take to drown if she rolled over.

She did not roll over. She splashed herself with water and the water pooled in the creases of her body and for a moment she imagined that I was still inside her and that my father was not Fitz but Jack Brown and it was Jack Brown, not the old man, on the other side of the bathhouse cleaning her saddle.

*B*y day, the forest was flush with the smell of wattle and the smell of honey. Jack Brown veered off the track and pushed into the dense mesh of trees and bright yellow flowers that exploded into dust when he passed them. Soon he was covered in their pollen, and their scent masked the stench that he carried in the sack behind him. As he rode, he could see new life poking up from the earth, the forest seeding itself in anticipation.

He nudged his horse forward until the bush was too thick to ride any farther and then he dismounted and tied his horse to a branch. He walked in, carrying the sack, counting tree by tree until he found the tree he was looking for. The hollow tree was his hiding place. Whenever he was paid by Fitz, which was not often, he rolled up his money like cigars and rode into the forest and deposited it in a tin he had lodged within the tree. When he first discovered the tree he thought to himself that the hollow was big enough for a body. But it was only a term of measure; he did not imagine he would ever hide a body within it.

He knelt down in front of the tree and took out his knife and used it to pry back the shield of bark that covered the hollow, just far enough so he could get his fingers beneath it and dislodge it. The bark came away and he felt inside the tree for his money tin, which was wedged above a knot. The tin had grown rusty and would not easily open, so he forced it with the edge of his knife. He took out a wad of notes and stuffed it into his top pocket, then he set the tin back in its place and heaved the sack into the hollow. But the sack was unevenly weighted and fell out of the opening of the tree. Jack Brown pushed it with his boot and then he pressed the bark into place, tapping it with the handle of his knife until it was all perfectly sealed.

Jack Brown did not know the intricacies of the law, but he did know that if there was no body, there could be no murder.

He collected his horse and found his way back onto the track. He rode recklessly, craving the sharp and certain guilt of murdering Fitz himself rather than the blunt feeling that he had failed himself and, worse, that he had failed Jessie.

When the river was in sight he cleared the fence that bordered the forest and the riverbank. His horse slid down to level ground and he clung to it while it regained its feet and then he rode it into the swell of the river, pushing it farther and farther against the current until he felt himself pummeled by the force and the coldness of it, and he wished that one day he might be cleansed of every old and acrid thought that clung to him.

～●～

I HEARD HIM charging around the river. His horse was brimming with sound and he was talking anxiously to it, as if he was trying to calm his horse and himself at once. My own heart leapt. There I was, waiting for my mother, and though he was not my mother, he surely could have been my father. And I thought anything she loved or longed for would do. Together, we could find her.

I called, *Jack Brown, I am not dead!*

I did not scream it else I be confused with those white-breasted birds that caw all day. I just called it as clear as I could: *I am not dead.*

As Jack Brown grew nearer, I wormed my fingers into the dirt above me. I knew my arms would not reach the surface but I thought at least I could fright his horse and then his horse might shy or, better, buck him right off, and Jack Brown would have to face the wonder of the earth moving beneath him.

With the weight of them upon me, I pushed harder into the dirt.

But both horse and man moved over me and neither was at all disturbed by my calling out or pushing at the ground above me.

*T*he dog's barking woke my mother early and when it stopped she heard the old man and the old woman arguing and then the old man call the dog, mount his horse and gallop off.

She took her time getting out of bed, to avoid the old woman. She dressed in clothes the old woman had given her and for some time she just sat on the bed. The small, windowless room reminded her very much of prison and she wondered if she would always feel that every room, regardless of how small or bare or not, was designed to punish her.

She opened the door.

The old woman was sitting at the kitchen table with her back to her.

Morning, said Jessie, and she filled the kettle with water, acting as if things were somehow normal and that she was a guest after all.

The old woman acknowledged her with a nod, though her eyes remained fixed on the window. She was peeling apples with a small paring knife and the peel curled into her lap in a long, unbroken twist.

You're good at that, said Jessie.

Trick is not to try, said the old woman.

She was distant and my mother preferred her that way.

Where's the old man? said Jessie.

He's in one of his dark moods again.

And why is that?

You're best to ignore him. He'll be gone all day, looking for some company for his misery. Though he won't have to go far for that.

The old woman began coring the apples. She had a hardened look about her.

Are there any of his chores I can do with him away?

No, dear, said the old woman, pinning back her hair, which was falling around her face. *For better or worse, that old man leaves nothing unturned or untended. Our most important chore for the day is to bake this pie and eat it. We'll eat it all and leave him nothing. And let's see if it doesn't restore us in some way.*

Jessie had not had the company of a free woman in years and she wondered if this was what free women did: baked pies and ate them to lift their spirits. She could see no harm in it.

She poured herself tea and watched the old woman coring the remainder of the apples and then slicing them and sliding them across the length of the table. She sprinkled each one with salt and sugar and vinegar and then she wiped her hands on her dress, shuffled over to the sitting room and pulled open the lid of a desk. Out popped a gramophone.

The old woman dragged a box out from under the desk and picked out a record. She placed it on the tray of the gramophone and lined up a needle and then wound the thing up until music played.

Most days, she said, *I know I would be happier without him.* She moved back to the table with a new lightness of step and threw cups of flour into a bowl and tossed it through her fingers.

What is this we are listening to? asked Jessie.

It's Debussy's "Reverie," said the old woman, then she continued. *He was different when I first met him. But the years have not been kind to him and he is not the forgiving type, not at all, and there are some things I have done in my life that I wish I hadn't and he has found them unforgivable. And one of them has been the fact that I could never birth a healthy child. He is a superstitious creature, a stupid old man, and he thinks my womb is sour. Though he wouldn't know a thing about it.*

As she spoke the old woman kept adding things to the bowl— more salt, more sugar, lard and spices—until she was turning over a soft dough in her hands. And then she rolled it out with a glass jar and stretched it over a pie dish and layered it with apples and bustled around the kitchen, piling up the wood in the stove.

Jessie found it all mesmerizing, the music especially. She had heard big bands, trumpets and drums play carnival music, but this was different. It was gentler, unfolding in layers of sound. She did not know why but she felt like weeping and she bit into the enamel cup to stop herself. She wondered why she had found the old woman so distasteful at first and why things of beauty made her so sad.

Jessie did not at first notice that the old woman had gone but just as she did the old woman reappeared with a pair of boots.

Here, she said. *Put these on. There is something I want to show you.*

The old woman charged outside and Jessie followed her up towards the first ridge that overhung the property.

The old woman scrambled over the incline and the ledges until they came to a place where three rocks were lined up in a row, each with a small cross carved into it.

Beneath those rocks are my babies, said the old woman. *I couldn't carry any of them for long. I could carry those rocks up a cliff face better than I could carry the babies. My body got to a certain stage each time and then expelled them. Except for this last one—I held him in my arms for three days. I called him Jude, after St. Jude, the hope of the hopeless. I thought, if Jude cannot save him, nothing can. And Jude could not save him.*

I'm sorry, said Jessie.

When I was younger, about your age, I spent days and weeks and months up here, praying for their little souls, praying they were not lost in limbo. Because limbo is a terrible place, it's like a void for the soul.

Do you dream of them? asked Jessie.

Sometimes. Sometimes they are babies and sometimes they are fully grown as if they survived to be good strong adults and it is me who is in their arms, it is me they are holding. The old woman laughed. *But that's just dreams, isn't it?*

W hen the old man returned in the early evening his mood seemed improved. The old woman fussed about him, hand-feeding him and massaging his feet. Jessie was surprised at the change in the old woman but she guessed this was her way of restoring some peace between them. He did not say where he had been and the old woman did not ask him. Jessie watched the old man's mouth uncrease as he relaxed and his eyes roll back in his head. She did not trust him.

The old woman had put the gramophone away when she heard the sound of the old man and the dog moving up the hill and now the only sound was the wind hurtling down the mountains and the spitting of the fire, which Jessie tended.

There'll be another storm tonight, the old man said. Jessie did not care for an evening filled with the old man's pronouncements but soon he was asleep in the chair and snoring.

The old woman said, *There's no point in moving him* and she wrapped herself in a shawl, put her hand on Jessie's shoulder and said, *Night, love. Best sleep with a pillow over your head 'cause this one's snore can travel through walls.* Then she left my mother sitting by the fire.

Jessie stoked the coals against the unburnt wood and wondered where exactly the old man had traveled to that day, if he had caught word of Fitz's death, if it was thought to be an accident, if she was deemed to be missing or dead. The wondering made her anxious.

She knew she had recovered well enough now to head up into the mountains but she must choose her moment so as not to attract more suspicion or bad feeling. She pulled the grate over the fire. She thought a way out might come with sleep and she tiptoed towards her room. As she was moving past the old man he began making choking noises that woke him. He sat up. For the first time he looked like a frail thing to her, clutching at the sides of his old chair.

He was panting. *Be good and make an old man a cup of tea*, he said.

She made a weak pot of tea for him, thinking she did not want to keep him awake, and she set the pot in front of him with a mug.

He said, *Where's yours?* And: *Keep an old man company. Pour one for yourself.*

Jessie poured herself a small amount and sat cross-legged again in front of the fire grate.

The old man narrowed his eyes at her and the effect was menacing, although she suspected that his sight was fading and this was the only way he could focus.

Where did you ride today? asked Jessie.

It's me who should be asking the questions, said the old man.

Go ahead, then, she said, and she hoped he was shortsighted after all, because she could feel the effects of her anger already playing out on her face.

Where have you come from? said the old man, sitting forward on his chair.

Sydney originally, she said. *Just passing through. Just another woman down on her luck is all*. She sipped the tea and kept her eyes downcast.

Down on your luck, eh? Yes, it seems you are, said the old man.

No use in dwelling, she said, and she stood up. *I'm heading out the back to get more wood.*

She grabbed the old woman's coat from the back of the door and she heard the old man call out something after her, but she did not care to hear it. It was a relief to step away from the house, to make her way across the yard and through the dark to the woodshed.

The woodshed was neatly stacked with kindling and short stumps of wood that the old man spent his days chopping and piling. She stamped heavily on the ground in the old woman's boots to give warning to snakes or spiders that she was entering their premises.

Standing at the entrance, she heard Jack Brown's voice, as clearly as if he were standing behind her: *If not now, then when?*

Was this the time to escape?

As she moved into the shed and collected wood she answered herself: *Girl, you won't survive long in the mountains without a knife and a gun.*

With wood stacked up to her chin, she moved back down to the house. She could see the old man through the window, watching her.

That night, as the old man had warned, a storm did break and it brought down trees. Jessie lay awake, listening to the trees falling and splitting and the strange bracketing sound of one tree catching another.

And then she slept, fitful with dreams. When she woke in the morning, there was only one that she remembered.

Septimus, her father, was sinking down and down.

Jessie could see his whole life floating up. There were women swimming around him, their eyes beaming light, a three-legged dog, a clock he kept time with, trees they had hidden behind in the woods, all floating up around him like leaves in a cup. Her brothers and sister appeared one by one, phosphorescent creatures.

Septimus tried to reach out to them, tried to take their hands, but they looked horrified by him and they beat their arms and legs to get away from him. And the women, with their bright eyes and billowing silks, tied their skirts into knots so he could not get hold of them.

But my mother had been there all along, swimming beside him, offering her small hand.

Jessie?

Dad.

My darling, he said. *Now is not your time to die. You are free. Now go!*

*J*ack Brown rode on to the Seven Sisters. He rode beneath the tin sign that hung from a beam nailed to two wooden posts. The breeze was behind it and the sign made a sound like a single bird cawing across the paddock.

It read: *7 SISTERS. BATHS & SHOWS DAILY*

Jack Brown kept his horse at a quick stride, moving along the sweep of ochre-colored road until the Seven Sisters was in view. It was a two-storey house with a huge center window that was lit up with colored lights. The lights dangled from a sign that said OPEN ALL DAY ALL NIGHT. This day there were twenty or so saddled horses lined up in front of the house, their necks straining into a drinking trough.

Jack Brown needed a shave and he needed a bath. He imagined that after riding so far he had collected every kind of northwestern pollen and every kind of northwestern dirt. There was a line beneath his knees, a watermark, where the river had washed his trousers part clean.

He galloped up the last stretch of road and tied his horse alongside the others, then he leapt up the steps to the house.

A girl with bright orange hair opened the door. He had not seen her before. She had red-painted lips and she was wearing a brilliant green dress, which, all combined after the long ride, was like a shot of color waking up his senses.

I'm here for the usual, he said.

Usual? There's nothin' usual around here.

A bath and a shave, said Jack Brown.

Are you black? said the girl, examining him. *We don't serve blacks.*

Jack Brown felt that familiar and exhausted anger. *Where's the madam?*

She's off crook. You look black but you've got blue eyes, said the girl.

And what color do you think I am inside? said Jack Brown.

The girl looked confused. She did not answer.

Tell Lay Ping I'm here. I'm a regular.

Do you have money? said the girl.

Jack Brown pulled a wad from his pocket.

S'pose you're not too black. It's just with them black ones you never know if they've got money to pay.

I'm an Irish bastard, just like you, he said.

The girl stepped back from the door and Jack Brown walked inside.

On the wall behind the front desk was an arrangement of strings that wound up to the second level of the house. Jack Brown had never been upstairs but he guessed that somewhere along the hall the strings split off into the rooms where they were each connected to a bell. The girl pulled on one of the strings and soon Lay Ping appeared at the top of the stairs. Jack Brown could feel heat radiating from his face at the sight of her. She was holding the banister as she walked and her dress was so tight, all the way to her ankles, she could only walk down the steps by twisting her hips from side to side.

This man says he's your regular, said the girl to Lay Ping.

Jack Brown stood up.

Lay Ping put out her hand and said, *Jack Brown. So dusty!*

Jack Brown took her hand. *I'm hoping you can clean me up, make me respectable.*

I tried that before but it did not work!

They both laughed.

Can we try again? said Jack Brown.

No time, said Lay Ping, *I am star of the show. But you wouldn't know because you've never seen it.* She punched Jack Brown on his shoulder. *I can give you a shave*, she said. *And maybe if you stay after the show, I can make you respectable.*

Lay Ping led Jack Brown through two swinging doors into a room signposted THE WET ROOM. The room was steamy and thick with the smell of tobacco and the menthol of shaving cream. Lay Ping sat Jack Brown in a reclining leather chair. Standing behind him, she tipped him and cupped his chin with her hands and scraped her fingers through the thickness of his beard.

You want it all off? she said. *Or you want those lamb chops?*

She traced a line beneath his cheekbone with her finger.

What do you think?

I don't like them.

Whatever you think is best, Lay Ping.

Lay Ping covered Jack Brown's face with a hot towel and pressed her fingertips into his temples. She wrapped her hands around his head and drew her hands in and massaged the hinge of his jaw. Soon he was aware only of his skull on his neck and his mouth gaping open. She ran her hands through the hair on his head and pulled at the roots, which sent a tingling from his scalp to the soles of his feet. He felt a suction on his forehead as she drew breath through the towel and then she thwacked him on the head and it sounded like a hammer, though it did not hurt at all. She unwrapped the towel and replaced it with another that was hotter and smelt of eucalyptus and made his eyes water.

She removed the towel and worked up a lather against his jaw, moving the brush in small circles into his beard, and then she began to shave him, flat blade from the neck. She scraped the blade up and over his chin, his cheeks and the dent between his nose and his lips.

And then she did it all again.

His skin felt like it was finally breathing air, not dust.

She patted him with a warm, soft towel and then she whispered into his ear: *Jack Brown, time for show. Will you watch me?*

Jack Brown had not planned it; beyond cleaning himself up, his single purpose for the day was to visit the police sergeant. But now he was in no mood to ride off suddenly.

Let me make your mind up for you, said Lay Ping. *You will stay.*

Whatever you think is best, Lay Ping, said Jack Brown.

Lay Ping led him out of the wet room and through the entrance hall and down a corridor to a single door.

Go through, she said. *Maybe I see you later.*

He opened the door. It was a side entrance to a large hall.

Within the hall were the owners of the horses, twenty men or more, and Jack Brown could smell them better than he could see them. The lights were dimmed right down and as he walked along an aisle to find a seat he could smell the stench rising from their torpid bodies. He wondered if, below the neck, he smelt the same. No man acknowledged him. Their eyes were fixed ahead on the red curtains, which rippled with the promise of women behind them.

Jack Brown sat down in a seat three from the front and cast his eyes along the row of men. He thought it was curious how none of them were speaking to one another, how they were all looking ahead, only the jangling sounds of a piano saving them from their own silence.

When the lights went down and the curtains drew back, the men shifted upright and to the edge of their seats. Jack Brown felt the row tip forward with the weight of them. The men broke from their silence, clapping their hands and stamping their feet on the boards. One by one, women appeared onstage dressed in silver smocks that showed off their legs and shoulders. The pianist played a more melodious tune and the women danced, arms linked, around the stage. Each woman took the hem of another woman's smock and drew it up more and danced in circles, six women in each, revealing the tops of their thighs as they turned. There were three circles and they merged like petals forming a flower. Then the curtains were drawn again and the men stamped their feet and yelled for more, more, more.

When the curtains reopened, the stage was filled with something like smoke, although it did not smell of burning, and the women pitter-pattered out and formed circles again and merged into a flower. Then they slowly sank down as a woman in a feathered mask rose from among them and stretched out two silk wings. The only thing covering her breasts was a sash. A half slip draped from her hips.

It was Lay Ping.

The men drew breath as the women rose again, concealing her. The women made a line at the front of the stage, their shoulders touching, and then they split to each side as Lay Ping danced, her sash edging slowly from her breasts and slipping down her waist until it was caught by her hips. Her wings were outstretched.

Lay Ping fluttered her wings and danced until the women returned bearing pitchers. Then they stood in two lines either side of Lay Ping and each woman took a turn at pouring water on her shoulders. The water trickled from her breasts in curving streams and a man in the audience yelled out, *I'm thirsty*, and then all the men laughed as one.

But they fell silent again as the water soaked into Lay Ping's slip and revealed the darkness between her legs. She brought up her wings and twisted her shoulders until the wings fell to the ground. Then she turned her body slowly until she had her back to them.

Jack Brown had never seen Lay Ping's bare back. But here it was, a perfect back covered in tattoos. From a distance, it looked to him like the window of colored lights with its sign that said OPEN ALL DAY ALL NIGHT, only here, in the only pale space remaining between her shoulder blades, was a single word, SORROW.

As he read it the other women ran in and folded around Lay Ping. Then the curtain was drawn and the music reached a crescendo.

Sorrow.

It was still on the men's lips as they sat in the darkness of the hall and it was still being whispered around as the front doors were opened and the daylight swept in.

On either side of Jack Brown, some men sank into their seats while others stepped right over him to get out. He did not move from his seat.

As the men departed, dust poured in through the open doors of the hall and covered the men who had saved their money to stay. Jack Brown decided then, like any free man, that at last he should be one of them.

*M*ore days and nights passed with the sounds of the storm and the sounds of the dog and the forest and the old man and old woman arguing. Jessie was biding her time. She tended to Houdini when she could but most of her energy was spent keeping out of the old man's way.

She could not collect supplies for her escape as there was nowhere to hide them, so she spent nights mapping their location in her head and charting the surest, fastest way to move through the house, to the stable and then away.

Early one morning she woke to silence. She did not understand why the silence sounded so vast until she realized the storm had finally died down. The cottage was utterly quiet.

She lay there for some time, recalling the map to her mind, knowing the time had come and she was about to launch herself out of bed when she heard the door of her room open. Her skin bristled as she saw the silhouette of the old man moving towards her.

She lay perfectly still as he stood squarely over her. And then her hand rose quietly in the dark and even her fist hitting his jaw was quiet and her legs swinging out. It was the sound of his head hitting the chair that finally made an awful crunching.

She did not care what damage she had done. She shut the door behind her and moved into the kitchen, collecting from the cupboards and the drawers a knife, a gun, a packet of matches, apples, the old woman's coat, the old woman's boots. The feeling of escape was familiar and she did not care to feel it again and so soon.

She set everything onto a tablecloth and then bundled it up. She was tying it to her waist when she noticed the old woman standing in front of the fire.

Go, the old woman said.

The old woman stood as solid as a statue. Jessie could not clearly see her face in the dark, only her white hair, which was luminous. Jessie felt locked in her view and she did not move until the old woman raised a trembling hand and pointed to the door.

I'm sorry, said Jessie, and she pushed out into the yard and up to the stable. She mounted Houdini and rode out. She rode up the steep slope and did not look back. She could not tear straight up the mountain in the dark so she zigzagged as far and as fast as she could. The bundle loosened on her waist and she wrestled with it as she rode, tying it tighter, prizing all of its stolen contents. She steered Houdini by his mane and felt a strength pulsing through her arms and across her chest, as if her body was remembering itself as she rode.

As soon as the sun tipped the horizon she tore up the slope. It was only when she reached a solid ridge that she dared to look back down into the valley.

There was no sign of any human presence and she could not see the old woman and the old man's cottage or any other hut. Below were empty fields but for clusters of trees and the river. The river stretched south and wound its way across cleared paddocks, a measure of how far she had come.

III

*T*he earth, as I can feel it, is pressed together at points and ruptured in parts. And so events seem to fold into one another, like burial and birth. It's not like the smooth and undulating beauty of a ribbon streaming out. No. The earth buckles with the stories it holds of all those who have cried and all those who have croaked.

The dying began in 1903 when my mother was nine and then it happened again in 1904 when my mother was ten. No dream or nightmare could have prepared her.

Life until then was riding horses in and around the woods and climbing trees and at night lying in her bed and sending out love from each side of the single chalk line that divided her. The horses were real and so were the trees but the chalk line was a thing in her head, though she saw it clearly enough, running over her body and over the bed, and she slept knowing that equal parts of her were apportioned to the two people she loved most, her father and Mrs. Peel.

They lived in Mrs. Peel's house—Septimus, Aoife and the five children. As a single man, Septimus had boarded with the widow, Mrs. Peel, and kept her gardens and set up his blacksmith business in her back shed. She welcomed Septimus's burgeoning family and became like a grandmother to them, midwifing each one of them.

Jessie did not know how, as adults, they divided their love among five children but she felt their devotion wholly: Mrs. Peel performing all of the duties under the sun, seeming to overflow with a bottomless well of devotion, and Septimus working every day from his shed to feed and clothe them. Each afternoon he would take a break from his work to lead a procession into the forest, a procession of children running after creatures and collecting pinecones or taking turns at riding on their father's shoulders.

Through all of it, Aoife slept. Her room was a fortress and the children were forbidden from knocking on the door or entering. It seemed to Jessie that her mother had slept for most of her life and when she did appear, pale and tall and shifting around the kitchen, she was always groggy or annoyed and Jessie knew better than to bother her.

The household ticked over well enough even with Aoife's occasional appearances. Most days and nights they forgot she was there. Mrs. Peel sat at one end of the table and Septimus sat at the other and Jessie felt that the world was at least in perfect balance, if not in perfect harmony.

One winter morning the children were slinking around the table in their pajamas but there was no breakfast to eat and there was no Mrs. Peel. The two older boys were already out and working with their father, which left Jessie and her sister, who was older by a year, and their little brother, who was four. They raced to Mrs. Peel's room and, pushing open her door, found her sitting upright in her bed, her mouth agape and her teeth in a glass beside her. Her eyes, too, were wide open.

They climbed on her bed to wake her from her open-eyed sleep but though they tugged and pushed her she did not stir but fell sideways. Jessie's sister screamed.

Septimus appeared and ordered them to get down from the bed. They watched as he put his head to Mrs. Peel's chest and his fingers to her neck. Then he sat down beside her and pushed her eyelids shut. He turned to face the three of them. They were swinging from the brass ends of the bed. *Children, Mrs. Peel has passed on.*

Passed where? they said.

I'm afraid Mrs. Peel is dead.

Until then, Jessie had not known that anyone could die or anyone could leave her. Her father's words left her with a lopsided feeling. It was as if one half of her was just a dull outline in the air and the other side of her had vanished completely.

It was less than a year after Mrs. Peel's death that Jessie woke to hear a rattle and a groan from the direction of her father's shed. She lurched past her sister's bed to the window. Outside, Aoife was wheeling what looked like a body slumped in a barrow. Jessie ran past the other bedrooms and into her father's room. Finding his bed empty she ran down the hallway to the back door and over the lawn to see her father's cart pulling away and weaving a terror up the road.

She ran after it and when she could not catch it she veered off the road and ran through her neighbor's paddock and caught one of the horses in their yard. She cantered back to the road and followed the tracks of the cart. She rode until she reached the outskirts of the city, until the dirt became bricks and pavers and the streets narrowed and there were people, strangers, stepping in and out of shadows, and there were no longer tracks to see or to follow.

One of the strangers stepped out onto the road and reached for the horse and said, *Little girl!* But there were no reins or bridle to catch and Jessie rode around him and around the streets until she was near lost completely. She knew at least the direction of the river so she rode until she reached it. She could see people were living in tents along its banks and the smell of open sewers was overwhelming. She rode on regardless, passing more tents, but there was no sign of people until she saw at last a footbridge and one tall, pale figure pushing a barrow. It was Aoife.

Jessie leapt off the horse and ran towards her. Closer, she could see the barrow was empty. She spread out her arms to block Aoife's way and said, *What have you done with our dad?* Aoife did not answer so Jessie grabbed her skirt and yelled again, *What have you done?* Aoife continued walking with Jessie dragging behind her but then she shook her off and Jessie fell against the wooden slats of the bridge.

Your father is dead, said Aoife.

You killed him, said Jessie. She could hardly speak the words. She was seething, delirious.

Get up, you stupid child, said Aoife. *Your father killed himself.*

My mother did not believe her.

She wedged her fingers between the wooden slats and gripped them as Aoife tried to pull her up to standing. Aoife quickly gave up on her.

Find your own way home, she said.

Jessie watched her push the barrow across the bridge, load it into the cart and drive away. There was no one on earth she loved less.

From the middle of the bridge all was silent but for the black and shimmering river lapping against the bank. Soon it settled and it was just a mirror reflecting stars and it looked to her like the universe had turned itself inside out and over.

Later, Jessie would dream that she dived in after her father. In reality, she sat on the bridge until the sun came up. Only then did she notice the horse was gone. So she walked along the riverbank until she spotted another. She did not care for any consequence, just flipped herself up onto the horse and tore along the riverbank. She rode in the direction of her house but did not stop when she got there. She kept going until she reached the woods and there she let the horse go and climbed a tree. After sitting in it all day and the next night she realized a terrible thing: her father and Mrs. Peel were gone because she loved them both too much and somehow that love had tipped the perfect balance of the universe. It had tipped things right over.

From Old Road the police hut appeared deserted. Jack Brown slowed his horse and examined the place from a distance. A blanketed horse stepped from behind the hut and turned in the holding yard.

Around him, Jack Brown could see the country from this side was swept clean. Winds buffeted the rise and, despite the recent downpour, the grass was a yellowy gray and the trees all had a bent-over and craggy look. Mostly, the view was trees and shadows of trees on empty fields. There were a few young eucalypts clustered near to the hut and their branches fell together like the fanning tail of a lyrebird.

Jack Brown eased himself out of the saddle and tied up his horse at the front of the hut.

He approached the hut slowly, stepping heavy on the ground, wanting to surprise no one. He knocked on the door, waited, knocked again and then peered in through a window at the front of the hut. He could see a man tiptoeing around in his socks.

Jack Brown sat on the wooden bench that ran between the window and the door and made scraping sounds with the heels of his boots on the boards so the police sergeant would know he was still there, waiting.

Soon he heard a bolt slide. The sergeant was at the door. Jack Brown stood up, took off his hat, offered his hand.

Morning, Sergeant, I'm Jack Brown.

The sergeant was a head taller or so than Jack Brown, but Jack Brown guessed they were about the same age, or maybe Jack Brown was older.

Sergeant Andrew Barlow, Barlow said and shook Jack Brown's hand.

Jack Brown noticed Barlow had put on his polished boots and police coat before he stepped outside. He had sparse blond sideburns and he had combed his hair down in front of his ears as if to make up for the lack of them. There was a city air about him. To Jack Brown he looked like some fop who had been dropped ill equipped into the valley and into the hut.

You're the first man I've met here so far, said Barlow. *Least the first one who's introduced himself openly. Mostly people have been running for cover when they see me coming.*

Don't take it personally, Sergeant, said Jack Brown. *Any policeman round here would find it hard to win favor.*

Certainly no one is bringing me hot dinners, said Barlow.

The two men laughed and Jack Brown could feel himself relaxing.

How long you been here? he asked.

Twenty-one days and counting.

About as long as my ride up north, said Jack Brown.

They stood in silence then, on the edge of the veranda, looking out into the valley.

What brings you here, Jack Brown? said Barlow finally.

I'm a drover for Fitzgerald Henry, said Jack Brown. *I'm just back from delivering his cattle up north, but on returning I discovered there's been a fire at his house and neither he nor his wife are there now and there are no neighbors to speak of, or none who would be concerned for their whereabouts. So, Sergeant, I'm not really sure why I am here, whether it is to report them dead or to report them missing.*

Barlow's eyes lit up. *Have you had a good look around the house?*

I have, said Jack Brown, and as he said it there were feelings welling up in him and he did not know what to do with them. He found it easier to look out towards the valley as he spoke rather than to look Barlow in the eye. *I found no sign of either one of them. There are some horses in the stable, but many are missing and there is cattle still wandering all over his property.*

Were there children? asked Barlow.

No. Or rather none yet.

Yet?

Jessie was pregnant.

Jessie? said Barlow. To Jack Brown's surprise Barlow put a hand on his shoulder. *Jack Brown, it is right you are here because this is much more than one man can handle.*

Right, Sergeant, said Jack Brown. He was relieved to have a partner in it all.

Will you ride there with me? said Barlow.

Of course. It's about half a day's ride.

You lead, said Barlow.

❧

THEY SET OFF down Old Road, Barlow's horse freshly saddled, Jack Brown's watered and fed. From the outset the horses they rode were not in synch; Barlow's horse was edging out in front of Jack Brown's and Jack Brown thought it was better not to irritate the man or his horse. He pulled back.

Do you know where you're going? Jack Brown said to Barlow.

No, said Barlow, *I'm off the map.*

Cross the field. You'll get to the river. Then follow the river to the forest, then head into the forest. You'll see a track. Keep on it till you got to the other side.

They steered their horses off Old Road and leaned into the field. The grass cracked against the legs of their horses and within the grass Jack Brown could see the ribs of cattle but it did not slow them. Both men's horses slewed across the paddock, kicking up dirt and bones, neck to neck, Jack Brown's horse hedging Barlow's.

*T*hey moved like apparitions, shifting in swathes of red in the distance.

Jessie pulled up her horse. There was a woman, her skirt draped over her arm in a bundle, and a man wearing a jacket with tails that flew out as he walked. He was twice the width of the woman, even with her carrying the bundle.

Jessie was twelve years old. By then she cared for nothing, nothing but pushing her lean body to the limits of itself, climbing higher and higher trees and riding recklessly. Every day Jessie launched herself onto her horse and tore across the paddock at breakneck speed. And when she was bored of charging back and forth, she'd flip herself around to ride seated backwards or push the horse to clear a fence and then turn it sharply to clear the fence again, zigzagging a course. She did not care for style or form, as long as she felt the air passing through her.

One day she rode the horse right up to the fence and, just before it jumped, she flipped her legs up along its back, as if she were flying.

They saw her.

Jessie regarded them from her horse but she did not ride towards them. She sat watching as they walked, as the details of their forms became clearer. The sun caught the gold threads of the man's jacket and he glimmered in patches. Jessie shielded her eyes from the glare of it. The woman wore a headdress, though it might have been hair piled up on her head, with flowers and combs and feathers poking out of it.

Dear girl, called the woman, waving a lace handkerchief above her head. She was striding now, almost running towards Jessie.

My dear girl, we saw you riding. We're on our way out of town, but we had to stop and ask you . . .

The woman was near out of breath. Her cheeks were pink and her hair dripped in ringlets around her high forehead.

Ask me what? said Jessie.

Your name, darling girl. Your name and the age of you.

Jessie swung down from her horse and stood in front of them. *Why do you wanna know?*

Jessie was aware that her own hair hung around her shoulders in knots. She was barefoot and the clothes she wore were her brothers' castoffs.

Where is your mother? asked the woman.

Jessie pointed to the rusted roof of the house at the edge of the paddock. *She's over there.*

Through the kitchen window Aoife saw the couple and Jessie leading her horse beside them. The woman looked dazzling to Aoife and she was made even more dazzling in contrast to the neglected lawn and house. She slipped behind the cupboard to wet her lips, pinch her cheeks and push up the messy tendrils of her hair.

Hello, the woman called through the door. *Are you Jessie's mother?*

Who's asking? said Aoife, going out to meet them. *What's she done now?*

I am Miss Spangellotti and this is Mirkus, said the woman. *And we have had the good fortune of meeting your daughter.*

What could be fortunate about that? said Aoife.

We are forming a circus and we think your daughter could be one of our star performers, said Mirkus.

Jessie saw Aoife's eyes narrow.

Of course, said Mirkus, *we will offer you some compensation for the absence of your daughter.*

To make up for your loss, added Miss Spangellotti.

You know she is worth a lot to me, said Aoife.

If Aoife had asked any questions other than *How much for my daughter?* she might have discovered that Miss Spangellotti and Mirkus were both German and they were determined to tour Mingling Bros. Circus of the World to every city and town in Australia. But she did not care to know where her wild daughter was headed.

That afternoon, Jessie hugged her little brother but not her mother and she climbed into the back of the high-wheeled wagon. There was no one else to say good-bye to. Her older brothers and sister had already left home and were working in the city, her brothers as blacksmiths and her sister as a domestic. Aoife walked out to the front of the house holding her youngest son by the hand but he broke away and ran after the wagon.

Jessie waved to him and she thought to yell *Go home*, but she did not because they did not seem to be the right words to say. The dust from the road soon enveloped him and soon she was numb to all feeling.

On the edge of Fitz's forest Jack Brown unsaddled his horse, unstrung his swag and saddlebag and threw it all down. There was just enough light to pass them through the forest but Jack Brown convinced Barlow they did not want to arrive at Fitz's in the half dark and have to camp there all night among the unbroken horses and frightened cattle. It was easy to persuade Barlow. By the end of the day he was flopping around in his saddle and Jack Brown could see the circles under his eyes had grown darker over their ride.

Jack Brown was in a sour mood. He felt it coming on as they approached the forest. He had compromised himself, and the forest and all it contained reminded him of that. Cobbling together half-truths and worrying more for his own neck than anybody else's were not the actions of the man he had supposed himself to be. Why should he have to win his freedom with lies? And if he could actually confess it, what would the truth be anyway? *Sergeant, for three years I have been rustling horses and cattle for Fitzgerald Henry alongside his wife and over that time I came to love her, or at least I believed I did. Fitz was a brute and I did not have the courage to stand up to him and when finally I did have the courage the man was dead.*

Fitz had died by Jessie's hand, Jack Brown knew it. By escaping and leaving Jack Brown to find the body, Jessie had made him a suspect. And he knew now they were in the worst kind of bind. Their freedom was in competition.

Jack Brown tied up his horse and began to brush it down. As he did he watched Barlow out of the corner of his eye. Barlow was floating around the campsite with his jacket over his arm. He picked up a fallen branch and stuck the end of it in the dirt and then hung his jacket over it. He continued undressing, removing his shirt and boots, and unrolled his swag. Then with a great sweep he brought his arms up over his head, circled them down, pressed his hands to his feet and began breathing like Jack Brown had never heard a man breathe.

The sight of him made Jack Brown more uneasy than he already felt. Jack Brown believed he could tell a lot about a man by the way he handled his horse and how he held himself in the saddle, and after observing him over the course of the day, Jack Brown thought Barlow was plainly odd.

Jack Brown distracted himself by gathering up kindling and wood, and when he returned to the camp Barlow was leaning up against his own saddle on his swag, sipping whiskey from a cup. There was no fire and he had made no preparations for dinner. He offered a cup of whiskey to Jack Brown but Jack Brown refused it. An unskinned rabbit lay near Barlow's boots, a rabbit that Jack Brown had shot some miles back. He found himself freshly annoyed to see Barlow already reclining.

Ever skinned a rabbit, Sergeant? said Jack Brown.

Neither skinned one nor eaten one, said Barlow as he took a slurping sip. *This will be my first.*

Oh no, Sergeant, said Jack Brown, *this is my dinner. I'm wondering what you're having for yours.*

Barlow raised his cup. *You've got a good humor, Jack Brown.*

What about a fire, Sergeant? said Jack Brown. *You ever built one of those?* Jack Brown squatted down and began stacking small sticks and leaves.

There's the first star, said Barlow, ignoring Jack Brown's question.

Jack Brown did not need to see the first star and he ignored Barlow right back, bringing his attention to building the fire. He lit the kindling and blew on it till it flared up. He broke some of the longer branches against his knee and fed them into the fire. He felt a tinge of pleasure when the wind picked up and blew smoke into Barlow's face and Barlow groped for his shirt to shield himself from it.

When the fire was blazing, Jack Brown sat himself on the ground cross-legged to skin the rabbit.

Is that good eating, Jack Brown? Barlow peered out over his shirt.

You'll see, said Jack Brown. He took out his knife and, stretching out the rabbit, he cut a neat seam through the middle of it.

Barlow moved in closer to watch him.

Sorry, Sergeant, said Jack Brown, *but you're blocking all my light.* He thought, second only to regret, there must be no heavier load than riding with a man with no bush skills at all.

When the rabbit was skinned, Jack Brown held it up to the fire and the fire lit up its bones and translucent skin. He rested it on a rock and twisted a piece of fence wire into two brackets. He flattened out another piece between his palms and threaded it through the rabbit and then he pushed his boot into the burning branches, slung the rabbit between the brackets and kicked at the coals till the wind swelled their flames, and then he sat himself down.

How long have you been working for Fitzgerald Henry? asked Barlow.

Fitz? About three years in all.

Does he pay you well?

Sometimes he does and sometimes not at all. Jack Brown leaned towards the fire and caught some drips of fat from the rabbit in a bowl.

What keeps you there?

Jack Brown was glad to have something to do while he was being questioned, to prevent him from fidgeting and giving himself away. He took a tin of flour from his saddlebag and added it to the bowl and mixed in enough water to make dough.

Hard to say, Sergeant. When Fitz pays me, he pays me well.

Does he owe you?

Yes, he does.

The rabbit hissed on the wire and Jack Brown buried the dough in a bowl at the edge of the fire.

I've been watching you today, Jack Brown.

Oh yeah?

You're a good rider, said Barlow.

I don't know about that, Sergeant, but what I do know is that in the saddle you've got a style all of your own.

Barlow laughed but Jack Brown could not even force one. He felt only tiredness and hunger. Barlow poured Jack Brown a whiskey and this time Jack Brown did not resist it. He threw it back and it livened up his throat.

What does the wife look like? asked Barlow.

Depends on who you ask.

I'm asking you. But I can ask around.

Well, Sergeant, that there is a tricky question. She is the boss's wife, after all. So for that one you'll have to ask around.

When Jack Brown tried to cut the rabbit, he found the bones were so fine and there were so many of them it was not worth cutting. They ate from the same plate, a dented lid from a pot, and picked off the flesh from the rabbit, which was tender enough, sucked the meat from the bones and then threw the bones back into the fire. The damper had risen to a golden lump and they washed it all down with more whiskey.

When there was nothing left on the plate, the two men sat in silence. It was the kind of night when Jack Brown felt the whole world shrinking around him so there was only what was lit up by the fire. Soon Barlow was nodding into his cup and Jack Brown thought to stand to wake him but his own legs felt drunk. He could only get to his knees. So it was on his knees he decided to build up the fire. When it was licking at Barlow's feet and Barlow still had not stirred, Jack Brown yelled, *Barlow! You'd be best to get into that swag of yours if you prize your balls and don't want 'em to be singed by the fire.*

Barlow shuffled himself into his swag. He said, *Good night, Jack Brown,* and the sound of his voice made Jack Brown feel sober.

Jack Brown turned in to his own swag and lay on his side and watched the fire spark up against the darkness and light up the trees beyond it. He tried to think only of trees, tree after tree, scattered, in lines, just trees. But then Jessie was there, always there, stepping out from behind them.

What did she look like? How could he ever describe her without revealing himself? He could not say, *I have stared at her face across so many campfires, on so many rides. At a distance, it's a face that looks fierce with its sharp jaw and dark eyes given over to the horizon. But when you are standing close to her, and her eyes are on you, you feel that she can see what's inside you and she's smiling so you know she likes what she sees.*

How could he say, *I have known no better feeling.*

Jack Brown rolled onto his back and the world of the fire opened up as he looked above him. Patterns of stars seemed to orbit one another, dust orbiting dust. He closed his eyes against them and he saw the stars falling behind his eyes. He followed the stars into dark, shimmering pools and he found that the shimmering pools had no end.

WHEN JACK BROWN WOKE, Barlow was sitting near the fire making tea. He had the look of just being washed. His hair was combed flat to his head and his face was smooth and freshly shaven, which made the hollows under his eyes look darker.

Sleep tight, Sergeant? asked Jack Brown.

Not a wink, said Barlow.

Ground not good enough for you? said Jack Brown as he stood up and shook his swag.

It's the cold, Jack Brown. Gets right into my back.

You got a bad back, Sarge?

I took a fall when I was a kid.

Well, let's get you back on the horse before you jam right up and I have to carry you out of here.

As they rode into the forest the mass of the trees glistened with dew above them. They looked to Jack Brown like giant pools in the air and he did not know how they held together and how it did not all rain upon him.

*T*he first time Jack Brown ever touched Jessie they were on the way to a drove. There was nothing of circumstance that night to bring them together. The weather was warm. They were suffering no storm and there had been nothing exceptional about the day. They had ridden along quietly beside each other for days. And days before on other rides.

That evening he made a campfire and prepared their dinner. She went down to the river to wash herself and when she came back her skin glowed in the light of the fire and her eyes were bright. It was the first time he had looked at her that day, always she was riding out ahead of him. But suddenly there was a feeling in him and it felt dangerous. He knew that when a man has enough space and silence and time he begins to think anything is possible or nothing is possible at all. This day, all the space and silence had set him to daydreaming of her, although she was right there, if not right there beside him.

That night, when they settled down to sleep, he imagined what it would be like to be next to her, to press his chest against her back, to feel her skin. But there was no reason for it. No way of closing up that distance between them.

Until he did.

She was lying awake on her swag next to the fire. He moved in beside her. She took his hand and rolled to her side and held his hand against her chest. *Sleep now*, she said. But neither of them slept. He lay awake for some time, breathing into her hair. Eventually, he forced himself to close his eyes, only with the hope of dreaming of her, of finding something that would flow from dreaming into life.

And then it did.

In the morning she would not meet his eyes.

We cannot ever speak of this, she said.

My lips are sealed.

I mean it, Jack Brown. This can never happen again.

As you wish.

Do you know what Fitz would do to you? And you can guess what he would do to me. Our feelings cannot be worth both of our lives, Jack Brown. We will bury them. Right here.

He knew her words were true. There was only danger between them.

North and west the inland climate gave rise to black and white cypress and tumbledown gums of iron-bark. Jessie looked down from the high ridge. Around her were deep cliff-lined gorges, giant ramparts and then more canyons, more rock. There was wilderness as far as she could see. It did not end.

She had been riding for a week.

She had stepped Houdini up and over the ridges and escarpments, felt the weather change, the air dampening her skin. Ledge to ledge were animals she had seen before only as fleeting creatures—rock wallaby, quoll. Here, they did not flee. They were as still as rocks as they watched her.

She and Houdini wound farther up the mountain, crossing granite bands, observing that their ledges curved like cupping hands and contained clear pools of water from which she and Houdini drank. When she reached a large saddle of the range she dismounted and led him through. Sweeping over them was an arch of granite boulders and walking through she felt a reverence such as she had never felt.

She navigated her way by the sun, and where the forest grew so dense that it would not let the light in, there were plants on the ground that turned their heads to face the sun's direction.

At night, she took her cue from those same plants and her limbs relaxed and her head turned down against her own chest and she slept an exhausted sleep, and when the sun rose again she traveled with the compass of the shadow of the mountain.

Her peace did not last.

She was leading Houdini over a high ridgeline when her remorse caught up with her suddenly. In front of her, a spectacular basalt scarp revealed the stretched necks and seismic heads of mother, father and child, the same faces Jack Brown had first pointed out to her from a far, far distance. It pained her to see them and feel that he should be beside her and between them there could have been a child, his or even Fitz's. And there was no escaping it, not the longing nor its looming and ancient reminder, its head lifted up against the sky.

She missed that longed-for life as if it had actually happened— as if she and Jack Brown had won their freedom, as if I were born in perfect time and strong. Days and nights she had allowed herself to imagine the simple, gentle happiness of our life together. But it did not happen. Now it shadowed her like any other myth.

She rode or walked or scraped along, leading Houdini, sometimes Houdini leading her. It was as if her eyes turned in, seeking some clue, something that in the spit and struggle of living she had missed as to how things could have been different.

Her sleep was taken up with nightmares of Fitz, so day and night she was all but ricocheting off the walls of her past and the feeling was like prison but now the prison was herself. She pushed herself and Houdini up more treacherous slopes. Houdini stepped dutifully behind her, though he was slipping more and more. She had no appetite but was reminded to graze when he did, feeding on fern fronds that grew between the exposed roots of trees. Still, she was growing ragged.

When she found herself kneeling against a slope and surrounded by sharp-edged rocks, it seemed to her that if she had spewed out her insides that is how they would look.

*T*he first time Jack Brown rode into Fitz's forest was the first time he saw my mother.

Jack Brown had ridden his horse along the southbound track as the letter from Fitz instructed. The track had wound him through an open paddock and then into the forest, alongside the river. He moved through the forest till he heard the reverberating sound of kangaroos, their bounding noise traveling from every direction. Jack Brown pulled up his horse and halted on the track. He had heard stories of mobs attacking lone riders, although he had never seen it himself.

He lay down along the neck of his horse and a huge gray buck appeared on the track, then a dozen or so smaller roos bounded past. They traveled in single file, following the gray buck down to the river, clearing the fence line one at a time. Jack Brown had seen them traveling in mobs before, mainly across open fields, but there was something impressive about the agile way they negotiated the thick bushland without losing their order. He watched them until they reached the river and it was then that Jack Brown saw my mother, sitting on a rock ledge. She was so still he might not have seen her camouflaged against the rock if she had not sensed him near and turned around.

Who's there? she yelled.

Jack Brown was surprised to see any human form after so long and especially a woman. He dismounted and walked his horse up to the fence line. She was already climbing up the rise to meet him.

I'm Jack Brown, he said. *I am looking for Fitzgerald Henry.*

You're Jack Brown? she asked.

Yes, he said, *I've an offer of employment from Mr. Henry.* He tapped his top pocket.

I'm Jessie, she said, surveying him. To him she looked steely and confused. *Keep heading down the track then*, she said, *and follow it till you get there.*

She turned away suddenly and headed back towards the river.

Jack Brown mounted his horse.

Thank you, he called after her. But she was already gone.

He steered his horse to the track and rode slowly, wondering who she was, if she was some forest dweller, some itinerant, and if he could expect to see her again.

He had set off from Sydney, where he had been convalescing for two months in a boardinghouse for ex-servicemen. The mood there was depressive and he was glad to leave it. It was filled with soldiers who had no family or wives or girlfriends waiting for them and they could not work immediately due to whatever injury they suffered. There were some single rooms, which were coveted, but otherwise they slept in bunk beds in a large dorm.

On Friday and Saturday afternoons most of the men would try to forget themselves by donning their army uniforms and cruising the pubs for good-looking girls before closing time in the early evening. Most often, Jack Brown was not allowed in because of the color of his skin so this usually meant smoking cigarettes outside before his party moved along to one speakeasy or another, where anyone could enter. If they arrived somewhere to find it shut down they would set up in a park or close to the harbor, which Jack Brown preferred.

Some of them began to partner off with the girls. One of the girls took Jack Brown on as her special project and one Saturday night she brought along a girlfriend for him. He thought the friend was attractive enough. She had big green eyes and yellow hair that was cut into a fashionable bob. She called herself a modern woman and she invited him back to her one-bedroom flat in Kings Cross and they went out for a picnic and once to a dance and once to the zoo.

For her, a modern woman's best accessory was the hip flask she carried in her handbag. On the ferry ride to the zoo she swilled from the hip flask too many times. *Jack Brown*, she slurred, *I don't care if you're black, white or brindle*, and she stuck her tongue in his ear. He felt so repulsed by her he thought he might prefer to swim across the shark-infested harbor rather than spend the rest of the day with her.

Aside from that, the city women kept such a pace Jack Brown did not think there was any use in catching one or keeping one when he knew the city was no place for him anyway.

And so he replied by letter to Fitz's advertisement for an Aboriginal stockman, which he had found pinned up in the foyer of the boardinghouse. A couple of weeks later he received a letter from Fitz in return containing a hand-drawn map and instructions on how to find his property.

Jack Brown was nineteen years old and, aside from his years in the army and the stock work he had grown up doing on the property where his mother cooked and cleaned, this was his first real offer of employment.

After meeting my mother near the fence line of Fitz's forest he made his way again along the track. Soon she came bolting past. She rode bareback and slipshod, like a man. She was all bones, and her hair whipped up and she raised her arm, a wave and a salute at the same time, and Jack Brown could not have guessed how familiar that sight would become, and how often he would find himself trailing behind her.

*B*efore Jack Brown appeared at the window of the station hut, Sergeant Andrew Barlow had been standing in the washroom naked except for his coat.

The rain and wind had passed but the hut seemed to hold on to the cold and it shot through Barlow's feet like darts. He had been angling his jaw to the broken mirror, inspecting his shave between the reflection of the mirror and the reflection of the blade. It was as good as he had looked since he arrived there.

When his father proposed the country posting, Barlow had imagined a hut stark on a hill and the station had proved to be not much more than that. On first actual sighting, Barlow wanted to turn back, and if it had not been his father riding beside him, himself a senior sergeant, Barlow would have felt no shame in admitting that of all the challenges of life, he did not feel fit, mentally or physically, for this one in particular and returning to the city as swiftly as his horse could carry him.

But his father had a grip on him. It was the firm grip of guilt and Barlow wanted to redeem himself.

Barlow was a drug addict and his father knew it. The country air and the isolation were thought to be the solution and even Barlow believed that if he could see it through and find something in it to occupy his mind if not his soul, somehow the experience would make the best of him.

As yet, he had no idea what the best of him was.

His father hung around for a week to settle him in. Together they cleaned the place up and restored a garden that was eaten out by rabbits and overgrown with weeds. Mostly the purpose of his father's staying was to keep an eye on Barlow, to make sure that he did not fall back into his old ways. The day before his departure, he told Barlow he was doing him a favor when he searched through his bags and packs and supplies. Finding a stash of vials and syringes in a silver tin, he made Barlow smash them in front of him with a hammer.

It was not that Barlow did not want to be free from his dependence but he had found no surer way to relieve the back pain that plagued him, that came upon him without warning and lasted for days.

By habit and by design, Barlow's mind was nothing if not expansive. He was open to alternatives. He sought them out, and before he left the city for his new posting he met a supple woman from India with a red dot on her forehead who was gathering recruits in an opium den. After Barlow described the particular pain he was in, the woman taught him a series of stretches. Before they fell asleep like a couple of cats on large cushions, they practiced the postures together and she assured him they would bring him relief, immediately and in the future.

Barlow took up the routine with enthusiasm but when he demonstrated the series to his father one evening, he was surprised to find that his father became infuriated. He said: *Son, it is undignified for a man to be bending and stretching in that way, and dressed in his pajamas. If you have to do it, for God's sake do it in private.*

When his father finally left Barlow to his own devices at the station hut, Barlow again took up the routine. He performed it every day as the sun came up and as the sun went down. If he felt any twinge of pain in between these times, he stretched himself out on the table in the station hut and swung his arms over his head and dangled there until he felt each vertebra lifting and the slow relief of it.

After a week or two Barlow's mind felt clear and his body felt good. The crowded feeling of the city left him and he found within himself an unoccupied space. It was something he had never known. He turned his attention to methodical tasks and with his full focus he ordered and sorted the hut and delved into the files he had inherited from the former police sergeant.

The post had not been filled for almost a year and the files were layered with dust and crawling with mites. Barlow was unperturbed. He cleaned each file and read it, examining each criminal's photograph in detail and recording the faces to memory so he would know them if he saw them, perhaps even on a dark night.

In one of those files Barlow found my mother.

She was the only woman in his files, and aside from that her aliases intrigued him: *Jessie Hunt also known as Bell also known as Payne*. She had appeared in court on many charges of horse rustling, under many different names. He lingered over her file longer than anybody else's, staring at her image, unclipping it from the file, reading and rereading her history and the sergeant's notes. He was disappointed that she no longer had to report to the station every month since her marriage to Fitzgerald Henry. But why was the file still there?

He examined her photograph with his magnifying glass and used the information in front of him to sketch out a time line of her life.

Jessie, he said, *Jessie, Jessie, Jessie*, as if his words alone would conjure her.

*B*y the time she was fourteen her name was being chanted by crowds under the big top of Mingling Bros. Circus. She was the Amazing Miss Jessie. Every night it was the same: Mirkus, the ringmaster, announcing her, Jessie running into the ring, the crowds yelling out, *Miss Jessie! Miss Jessie!* as she launched herself onto the podium. Josephine/Joseph tying her to the wheel of fortune, the Caped Man cartwheeling in from the side, drawing his knife and aiming at her while Josephine/Joseph set the wheel spinning.

The Caped Man, knife in hand, would dash around the ring, brandishing his blade in the air as Josephine/Joseph gave chase. When they lassoed him, he would not stop running. He would slice the rope with his knife and throw the tail end of it into the crowd, who would be hissing. Josephine/Joseph would run back to the podium to spin the wheel. Then it was like this, always the same: the flung knife, the cackle, the bloodcurdling scream and the crowd whispering around, *Did he get her?*

He never did.

Josephine/Joseph would untie her and she would cartwheel to a horse; still dizzy from spinning, she would jump neatly onto the horse's back and flip herself into a handstand for a whole lap of the ring.

One night, after the show, as the crowd spilt out of the circus tent, a waif ran beneath the stalls, through the streams of light and dust and columns of shadows. He ran until he reached the end of the row and then, peering under the tent and seeing no one on guard, sprinted to the stables.

When Jessie reached for a clump of hay to feed her horse, she grabbed a fistful of the boy's shirt instead. She did not let go of it until she had pulled him right out of the feeder.

He was one of the filthiest creatures she had ever seen. Skinny legs and skinny arms and his head too big for his small shoulders.

Who do you belong to? she said.

When the boy said nothing, she thought him mute. But he was not mute, he was mesmerized. Here was the Amazing Miss Jessie. The star of the show. He had seen her on all the posters.

At last he said, *Miss Jessie.* And then he bowed.

Where is your mother?

I don't have a mother, he said. *I grew on a tree.*

You're not a fruit, she said. *Of course you have a mother.*

I don't, said the boy. And that was the truth of it.

What's your name then, kid?

My name is Bandy Arrow.

She laughed. *Who named you?*

I named myself. I'm a performer, just like you.

Jessie walked him out of the stable and into the light to take a good look at him.

A performer? What can you do?

I can show you my roundoffs and turns, he said.

Jessie watched as he launched his small body into motion. Blond hair like a flame, flame over feet, around and around he went and he did not stop until she told him to.

That was it. She was fourteen and he was seven and Bandy Arrow became my mother's pet, her sparrow. When the troupe traveled from town to town they sat together on the back pole wagon. Their legs hung over the edge, way off the ground. It was their job to watch for horses that strayed from the procession. From the back of the wagon their view was wide and when a horse swayed out into open country, they would launch off the wagon and chase it down, pounding the ground with their bare feet, feeling the grass against their bare legs, without a care between them.

Jessie and Bandy spent a year like this, more days running through open country than performing under tents. Some days they wore wigs, just for their own amusement, and took turns leaping off the back of the wagon to do circus tricks. Jessie did not know how the sight of this little boy running with a curly blue wig bobbing from his head could make her laugh so hard, but it did.

One day when Bandy was running behind, the wig fell into the dirt. Sitting on the back of the wagon, Jessie pointed to the ground and yelled after him. Bandy slowed his running and Jessie stood up. The wagon rattled on, turning up clouds of dust. Jessie could just see Bandy's hands coming up to his head before she lost sight of him.

The sudden distance between them gave rise to a terrible feeling in her. She yelled to him again and then she heard her name as if it were an echo. *Jessie! Jessie!*

She banged on the wooden panels of the cart for the driver to stop.

She leapt down and ran towards him. He was hobbling, blue wig in his hand, blood covering his knees.

I tripped, Jessie, he said. *I fell. I couldn't see you and I didn't know what was coming.*

Jessie lifted Bandy into the wagon and tore off the tail ends of her shirt to clean him. The rest of the day she cooed over him, making him rest in the back of the wagon, blankets rolled up behind his head for pillows.

That day, she chased down the straying horses herself. Running into those wide fields away from him was the loneliest feeling.

Soon Jessie would come to understand that day as a terrible premonition, when Bandy Arrow fell and faded from her view.

S ergeant Andrew Barlow thought of himself as a Man of Science. It was more than just his fondness for scientific props, vials and test tubes or his previous experiments in preparing opium. For him, it alleviated the pressure that was in him. It was the inherent discipline of it, the formulas, and he regarded it as another man might regard his religion. Barlow believed in gravity. Gravity helped him make sense of things. Every night as the sky opened up he knew it was gravity that was keeping the planets in orbit. And the days that he felt as though he might just float off the earth, he reminded himself of the fact of gravity. It consoled him.

Riding through Fitz's forest, it was gravitational forces that Barlow had in mind. From his study of Newton's *Principia*, Barlow knew well enough the pull that large planetary bodies had on one another. But until now, it had not concerned him what force humans, in distance or closeness, might exact on each other.

He was thinking of my mother.

His thoughts were interrupted by the sound of bellowing. He caught up to Jack Brown and they rode on the track side by side, listening out.

The sound was disorienting until they found the source, a cow with its head caught in Fitz's barbed-wire fence. They swung down from their horses and Barlow pulled a small pair of pliers from his saddlebag.

Jack Brown looked surprised at Barlow's initiative and he held down the cow's head while Barlow cut the wire from around it, and then they both stood back as the cow scrambled to its feet and took off down the track.

They rode out into Fitz's paddock, Barlow wondering how all of it—himself, Jack Brown, Jessie, a bellowing cow—could fit into an ordered universe of perfect pull, perfect force.

But arriving at Fitz's, Barlow was reminded of the catch in Newton's theorem, his deus ex machina. It looked to him as though some furious hand had swept in and in one violent blow crushed the house.

With Jack Brown's help, Barlow raked through the house, examined every surface. There were footprints leading in and out and Barlow concluded that a day or so after the fire the place had likely been ransacked, and if there were ever bodies to be found there, they had been carted away with the kitchen sink.

Life in the valley was grim. The place was full of desperate men and thieves. By Jack Brown's telling, many of them were ex-soldiers who had been given plots of land, but they were not farmers and they did not know the land or how to survive it.

In terms of finding Fitz or Jessie, there was little for Barlow to go on. The only way he knew how to approach the investigation was scientifically and methodically. He would begin by visiting every hut in the valley. He would piece together a trail. He could not guess, yet, what would be at the end of it.

It was Jack Brown's idea that they ride to the postmaster's hut, as the postmaster was the only person in the valley who knew what places were inhabited and what places were not. Arriving there, Barlow talked the postmaster through the fire and the disappearance of Jessie and Fitz. The postmaster seemed inspired and he began to make an elaborate drawing of individual huts. He had even begun to draw rooftops and chimneys when Barlow said, *Thank you for your artistry, sir, but an X on the page will do well enough to mark a hut.*

But, Sergeant, said the postmaster, *I am trying to show you that these are the huts I have delivered to and these are the huts I have not— the ones that in all my time have never received a letter or a telegram. And, sir, you can imagine what kind of man that is. Not used to visitors I would say. But the huts with the chimneys, shaded thusly, are the ones that I have seen lately blowing smoke. So you know there is something live in there and will perhaps be cautious and prepared in approaching the others that may not.*

May not what? said Barlow, confused by the postmaster's explanation.

Have anything live in there, sir. The winter always claims some.

And whose work is it to find them, or bury them?

Well, sir, said the postmaster, *unless they're receiving mail, it's not my work to do. Perhaps it's yours, Sergeant.*

Barlow paced in front of the postmaster's desk while he finished the drawing.

When it was done Barlow presented it to Jack Brown, who had been watering the horses. *It's a work of art,* said Barlow, handing him the map, *only I have no notion where to begin.*

Jack Brown smoothed it out across the horse's saddle. *Not bad,* he said. *The man is particular. For a start you can tell north by that ridge of the mountains. Over there are marked the plots given away to the ex-soldiers. But you see the river is over here. If you want to visit them all, you'll need to ride more or less in a circle. So, Sergeant, it won't matter what direction you set off in first.*

Jack Brown mounted his horse.

Where are you going, Jack Brown?

I've done what I can, Sergeant. I reported the crime, I took you to it, I delivered you here. Now the fact of it is that my boss has gone and he's left me unpaid and idleness does not suit me. I need to find another employer.

Barlow began to panic. He needed Jack Brown. He knew he could not negotiate the valley without him and he knew there would be nothing more derided or endangered than a cop alone. Or, he guessed, a black man. So at least they had that in common.

How black are you, Jack Brown? asked Barlow.

Jack Brown turned on his horse. *Are you asking me what caste I am, Sergeant?*

What I mean to say, Jack Brown, and I hope this doesn't cause a man offense, is are you black enough to be my tracker?

Jack Brown laughed. *What are you offering, Sergeant?*

Room and a wage.

What's the wage?

What does a man expect? Six or seven quid a week?

I'll ride to the first hut with you, Sergeant. And I'll consider it.

They had not reached the first hut when Jack Brown said, *Sergeant, for seven quid a week I won't get you lost. For nine, I'll track anything with feet.*

With the Great War came the Great Suspicion. It rolled into Mingling Bros. Circus of the World like a dense fog that clung to its stalls. Suddenly, there were no more crowds jostling outside to get in and those that did turn up came less to admire the performers and more to determine if the performers were not the enemy themselves.

The word was out—Miss Spangellotti and Mirkus were German. Patriotism in cities and country towns meant there was no place that would welcome them.

Regardless, the troupe moved from town to town in the hope there was somewhere that had not caught on to the spirit of the time. They tried novel things to bring audiences in, changing into their costumes by the side of the road and marching into towns with an elephant in the lead to create a grand procession. But most often by the time they reached the town their costumes were dusty and as they marched down the main street people eyeballed them from behind shop fronts or curtained windows. Some sent their children out to throw rocks.

It didn't take long before the performers, including my mother, were missing their cues. No amount of putting on a brave face or colored sequins could make up for their hearts no longer being in it.

The night a man in the audience threw a dead possum at Mirkus, it happened to be the most well-timed stunt of the evening. The dead possum hit Mirkus's shoulder and slid down his velvet jacket, landing at his feet.

Mingling Bros. was over. Mirkus and Miss Spangellotti called in the troupe: the Indian cyclists, Josephine/Joseph, Maximus and Minimus, the Russian dancers, the Spanish acrobats and Señor Donata. And, of course, my mother.

That's it, my friends, said Mirkus. *Let's lickety-split. Let's blow the whistle. Take your costumes and take your horses. And for goodness' sake, take care of yourselves. The people are going mad and I fear this is just the beginning.*

Everyone in the circus had a partner except Jessie, and this was evident again in their departing. Maximus and Minimus. The cyclists. Josephine/Joseph and Señor Donata. Jessie realized that she was the only one who would ride off alone. She thought of Bandy Arrow, her pet, her sparrow, who had disappeared one day as suddenly as he had appeared. No one in the circus ever spoke of him and she wondered if, in her loneliness, she had not conjured him then as she would like to conjure him now, an imagined and perfect friend.

After the demise of Mingling Bros., Jessie turned her hand to all kinds of things, and mostly they were other people's things and other people's horses. There was an industry in it, selling horses to the army for the war. Broken-in horses were in hot demand and my mother knew where to find them.

She was swift and efficient and, thanks to her circus days, she could pull off many disguises. She appeared in Parramatta Court half a dozen times with her different aliases—Jessie Hunt, Jessie Bell, Jessie Payne—but the evidence was usually already gone, being shipped across the seas.

Until it wasn't.

She was twenty-one years old when she was finally convicted.

By then she was a seasoned and well-regarded horse thief, and when the crime was too effortless she would raise the stakes for her own amusement. It was when she swiped two chickens after stealing a horse that she was captured.

When she snatched the chickens from their coop, they were sleeping. With one hand she held both chickens upside down by their feet, and with the other she twisted their necks to kill them. But things did not go so well in the dark: one of the chickens began to flap its wings and she dropped it and it made a fearful racket. Unfortunately for Jessie, the owner of the chickens and the horse was listening—lately his chickens had been preyed on by a fox. When he heard the sound of their distress he tiptoed out into the night poised to shoot with his rifle under his chin. He was surprised to see not a fox but my mother coming out of the pen. He waited until she tried to mount the horse again, this time with two chickens under her arms, and then he stepped out of the dark and pressed the gun against her back and said, *Lady, you're a goner.*

The man directed her, at gunpoint, to the police station. There was no one around in the middle of the night so he sat there, with the gun at her back, until morning. And then he stood over her, satisfied, as two policemen pushed her fingers onto a pad of ink and took her fingerprints. By the time the policemen got her into a holding cell she had smeared them with blue ink. She kicked and punched them and spat out insults.

We've got a wild one here, they said.

Before my mother faced the judge she did her best to make herself look neat. But even with her hair pinned up in braids, when she stood before the judge she could feel his judging eyes upon her and knew that he saw her every imperfection, inside and out.

For the judge there was nothing to consider. My mother had been caught in the act. He tallied up her sentence: twelve months for the horse, three months for each chicken and six months for the assault of the police officers, which he assured the court was lenient.

He said, *In giving this sentence, it is my hope that this young woman might grow virtue, like a virtuous child in her womb, and the law will claim its paternity.*

*H*er physical energy was almost spent but her mind was a flurry of memory and her memories were ceaseless. She sat down on a rock and squeezed her throbbing head as one after the other the memories rose up. And as if there were pincers in her head, she would try to snatch a memory as it rose, to determine if that was the fate-altering moment when things could have been different.

For one whole day she swayed back and forth on her haunches, tapping her forehead with her knuckles as if she might extract something from herself. But by the end of the day she knew only two irredeemable facts: she had deceived Jack Brown and she had killed Fitz. She did not know who she was to do either.

Houdini grazed around her and it occurred to her that she might be undernourished. She did not move from the rock but waited with her gun and eventually she saw a roo and shot it. As she did she recalled the fleeting moment when she could have shot Fitz and it would have appeared a perfect accident.

SHE HAD BEEN with him for almost a year. By then she had lost count of the times he had hit her and she had already begun fantasiz-

ing about her escape to the mountains. On this day he was demon-
strating to her how to muster and brand his cattle. He said he was
going to promote her, send her out on a ride. She had no skills with
cattle, or none that she had cultivated. She had a natural talent for
horses but cattle she found to be too stupid to care for. They reminded
her of Fitz—she did not know what dumb things moved them.

For the sake of peace she took Fitz's lead and they rounded up
half a dozen cattle that he had brought in. They were moving them
from a lower paddock and into the holding yard when a bull broke
from the herd. It charged out in some kind of fit and while Jessie
jumped the fence, Fitz held his ground and swung a rope over the
bull—but it was to no avail as the bull was fast and deliberate in
charging at him and pushing him against a fence post. Fitz yelled at
Jessie to get his gun from the stable and as she started to run she
realized she did not care if the bull killed Fitz or not. She found the
gun propped against the wall; knowing better than to run with a
loaded gun, she walked back to the yard. She could see Fitz crawling in the dirt and she aimed at him, but the bull tossed him up and
then up again and then the bull's horns seemed to twist right into
him and she thought that they had impaled him. She fired a shot in
the air to scare off the bull and the bull charged the gate. Fitz took
his chance and rolled under the fence and it was too late to shoot
him so she shot the bull instead, twice in the head, and watched the
bull fall back, its full weight upon itself, and die right there in front
of them.

Fitz was a mess. Jessie washed and dressed his wounds. Just
from feeling she could tell he had two broken ribs and his knee was

shattered. He insisted she stay and mind the farm and he left her with the same gun she had grabbed from the stable. With great difficulty, he mounted his horse, one leg completely straight. She handed him a full bottle of whiskey and then she did not see him for two days.

She should have escaped. She packed the one bag she had brought from prison, a green canvas thing that lived under her bed, and she filled it again with the soaps shaped as angels and birds that by now had gathered dust on the windowsill. She looked around her bedroom and around the house and there was nothing else in it that she valued. The only useful things now were a knife and a gun and her shirt and her trousers. She saddled Houdini and rode down into the forest, which was the only way out of there. When she cleared the forest, she would head to the mountains. She thought she would be safe there. But she was not even halfway along the track when she thought she heard a galloping horse and she feared its rider was Fitz so she turned Houdini around, as sharply and swiftly as she had set off, then put Houdini back in the stable and herself in the brown armchair that she despised. By the time she realized it was not Fitz she had heard in the forest she had lost her nerve.

When he did return he was blind drunk, like a bull himself, and full of talk of his bull wrestle and, worse, full of plans. He announced to her that he would bring in another rider and her and the rider would be his drovers, his lackeys, heist to heist, as more or less his droving days were over.

He said, *I'll get a black fella this time.*

And Jessie asked, *Is that because of his droving?*

But she did not even register his answer. She knew that to Fitz a convict woman and an Aboriginal man were as good as slaves.

Later, when she first saw Jack Brown in the forest, she could have told him there and then to flee. But she knew that without Jack Brown she would be left alone with Fitz and if she did not kill him first, it was unlikely she would survive him.

SHE DID NOT KNOW how much time had passed. She had skinned the roo completely. She wished that she could skin herself, that she could pare herself right back to bone and pull apart those bones and reconstruct herself again.

She lit a fire and cooked some of the meat but as the fire licked up she saw the carnage she had created and her appetite was gone. She was disgusted with herself and with the waste of it.

There was blood all over her.

She smothered the fire with dirt and spread out the fur of the roo on the ground and then she lay down on it and wept. She was inconsolable.

Jack Brown was nowhere within reach and he would never be. The pact to wait was not for the reason she told him, that they must choose the right moment to escape. She had asked him to wait because she was trying to muster the courage to tell him that the child inside her was not his, it was Fitz's. In almost six months she had not found the courage to tell him. At first she thought it could have worked, their escape to the mountains, man, woman, child, seeking freedom. But could he have ever loved a child of Fitz's? Or could she? Imagining Jack Brown was my father was the only way my mother did not find me a repellent thing. As I grew inside her, she did her best to blot out my nasty biology. But the truth remained. And the truth was awful.

I could not hold that against her, her fiction. Because in it there was a seed of truth. Jack Brown could have been my father and, like my mother, I would have preferred that he was.

My poor mother curled against the fur of the roo. She pulled it around her and then she said, *Hold me.*

And her own words surprised her. But the words kept coming:

Hold me.

Hold me.

Hold me.

And in their utterance, she did not have another thought.

In the morning the stench of the pelt was made real by the sun and she unrolled herself from it and peeled off her bloodied clothes. She walked silent and naked, leading Houdini, afraid of how much death was in her.

J ack Brown and Barlow traveled steadily north through the valley. When they sighted a hut they slowed their approach so the occupant would have notice of their coming. Even then, some men were waiting with their guns propped and loaded. Barlow held his badge high above his head and it had the effect, at least, of making the men lower their guns. Then they would ride evenly and slowly towards the huts with their occupants watching keenly.

One of the men had his trousers pinned up over a stump of leg and his hut smelt worse than anything Barlow had ever smelt before. The man claimed to have seen Jessie. As he told it: *She moved through the bush like some bitch or beast clawing at the ground and her hair covered her wild face and if I could have loaded this gun faster I would o' gladly shot 'er.*

They rode for three days with few words between them, visiting and marking off each hut on their northern stretch, both the huts that were shaded on the postmaster's map and those that were not. Barlow was grateful not to find any dead thing.

By the end of the third day, there was one more north-lying hut, according to the map, and it was the one that was closest to the mountain. It was growing dark quickly and they could hardly see, but Barlow was determined to get to it, so they pushed their horses on until Jack Brown warned Barlow that their horses could stumble in a rabbit hole and break a leg, so the sergeant finally agreed to stop.

Jack Brown lit a fire and Barlow used the firelight to write police notes in his book. Jack Brown did not ask what he wrote. For dinner, they watched the horses grazing near the fire while they themselves chewed on the leftover damper Jack Brown had made for their lunch. In the distance, Barlow thought he could hear the barking of a dog.

Jack Brown lay down on his swag and soon he was snoring. Barlow felt wide awake. Together the trees and the fire made strange configurations and Barlow looked out into them until some of the configurations seemed to be stepping towards him. He strained his eyes to see them, and then he recognized them. They were all the men he had memorized, all the men in his files. They were moving in on him, and circling.

Jessie was not among them.

When the sun finally rose, Barlow was relieved. He could see the base of the mountain and close by was smoke rising above the trees. They saddled up the horses and soon they were riding towards it.

The dwelling they approached looked more like a cottage than the huts they had previously visited. Hedged by roses, a stable on one side, sheds on its perimeter. As they rode up, a dog started barking, and when they saw an old woman emerge from the cottage to tie it up, they pushed their horses into a gallop.

The old woman was friendly enough and she nodded as Barlow

gave a description of Jessie and Fitz. She said she would be glad to see any woman around here, but she had not, not for some years, and as for Fitz, she said she was not one to remember names, only faces, and a ruddy-faced man could have been any one of the men she had seen around the valley for the last forty years.

The dog kept barking, which unsettled the horses, and the old woman could not quieten it.

We would appreciate some breakfast if you have any to spare, said Barlow. *We've been riding for days.*

I am happy enough to offer you food, said the old woman, *but I'd prefer if you eat it outside as my husband is not well. He has grown used to the racket of the dog, but I know other men's voices will wake him.*

The old woman moved towards the house and Barlow and Jack Brown sat on ledges of rock near the stable.

Jack Brown said, *We needn't eat the old woman's food*, and Barlow said, *It's a long ride back, Jack Brown, and I don't have the stomach for more of your damper.*

Soon the old woman reappeared with two bowls of warm oats and she sat down near Barlow and Jack Brown. But the dog got loose and took off down to the house and they all watched it jumping up and down and scratching at the door until an old man opened it.

The woman yelled out, *Go back to bed. You are not fit to be out.* But the old man moved towards them, ignoring her. He had a bandage around his head.

What's your business here?

Barlow stood up. *I'm Sergeant Barlow and this is my tracker Jack Brown and we've come by to ask if you have seen a man or a woman who have gone missing. The man is large and thick around the neck, his face is red and so is his hair, and his eyebrows knot together. The woman is tall with long brown hair and brown eyes and she is known for her horse breaking and her riding.*

The old woman scuttled around them nervously.

Can I get you more oats? And whispering: *Don't mind him, he's not the full quid.*

She was here, said the old man. *Come down to the house, I have something to show you.*

What are you doing, old man? said the old woman. *Stop making trouble.*

It is no trouble, he said.

Barlow followed him down to the house and into the bedroom. He reached under the bed and pulled out an enamel cup. He was careful to pick it up with only two fingers by its handle.

This here is the cup that she drank from. It will be covered with her fingerprints.

This is most useful, said Barlow. *Which way did she head when she left here?*

Like any desperate creature, to higher ground. I expect you'll find her somewhere up there on that mountain.

Jack Brown stayed outside with the old woman, who paced around the stables.

Do you smoke? she asked. *Could you roll me one? A thin one. I'm not a smoker.*

Jack Brown took out his tobacco pouch. His palms were sweating and the papers stuck to his fingers.

The old woman sat down on a hay bale and stared at the ground.

Was she here? asked Jack Brown.

The woman was silent. Jack Brown waited. The cigarette paper came apart between his fingers and trails of tobacco threaded across his hand. He brushed his hand on his trousers.

She was here, said the old woman finally. *We found her in a bad way by the river.*

Six months pregnant, said Jack Brown.

Seven by her count.

Seven?

It doesn't matter, said the old woman. *The baby did not survive it. Did you see it born?*

No, said the old woman. *The babe was already dead and gone when we found her.*

There was no child inside of her? said Jack Brown.

No, said the old woman. *She was empty as a bottle.*

Jack Brown crouched low to the ground. He pulled his hat way down over his eyes and lit the cigarette he had rolled for the old woman. He smoked it and smoke streamed out his nose as he clenched his jaw and tried to push down all the mournful sounds rising in him.

*B*y the time Barlow and Jack Brown were heading back to the station, Barlow's whole body ached and the sun had not warmed him. When they arrived at the station hut, it was dark again and Barlow was glad of it. It was a veil for his mood. Jack Brown put the horses in the holding yard and, inside, Barlow lit two lanterns and found a blanket for him.

When Jack Brown came in from the holding yard, Barlow threw him the blanket and said, *There's an empty cell. Make yourself at home.*

Jack Brown acknowledged him with a nod and disappeared into the cell.

Barlow sat down at his desk, between the lanterns, and he opened my mother's file again. The photo of her was no bigger than the palm of his hand, but it was enough to reveal her. He could see her eyes like smudges of coal, her jaw jutting out, the look of defiance. The more he looked, the more he felt that there was something live in it.

He lined up all his props—a sable brush, a pot of lampblack, glass slides, gummed paper, his magnifying glass. He put on his white gloves. Then he unwrapped the enamel cup the old man had given him. Dipping the sable brush into the pot of lampblack, he hooked his finger around the handle of the cup and began to dust it. The dust collected around the smudges of her fingerprints.

Suddenly, he felt full of life. He rolled out the gummed paper and pressed it over each print, collecting four perfect samples—three of her fingerprints and one, on the rim of the cup, of her lips.

From her file he took out the impression of her fingerprints. He lined up the gummed paper samples next to it and, using his magnifying glass, he compared them.

He had her. There was no doubt that each print was one and the same.

*B*y midmorning the sun was high in the sky and the bush was radiant, inexhaustible in the heat.

Within the mountains were streams that gathered up in gorges, following a predestined course, crossing narrow ridges of rock. Jessie dropped to her knees next to Houdini and drank from the stream. She did not cup water with her hands but put her face into it and drank, like any other creature.

She unwound the bloodied tangle of her clothes, dressed in them again, and then she lay down in the shallows and let the water wash over her and wash her clothes clean. The rushing stream collected her hair and she felt it against her scalp like fingers stroking her and then those same fingers twisted her hair and pulled at it and she knew then it was not water that had a hold of her, it was ghosts—Fitz, Aoife, Septimus, Bandy Arrow, me. Even Jack Brown, she felt, had sent part of himself out after her. All had scraped up the mountain beside her and, despite her pleading, would not leave her.

Drenched as she was, she pulled herself from the stream and led Houdini towards the ridgeline. She viewed the mountain range, and the highest, steepest slope within it. And although it looked thick with scrub, impassable, she mounted Houdini and rode in the mountain's direction anyway, determined to escape all the ghosts that trailed her.

IV

You must have seen the tracks all over the country. The imprint of birds and cows and horses and humans, crisscrossing one another. And that's just the top layer of dirt. Beneath it are layers upon layers of fossilized things and rotting matter that tell something different again. Because down here stories overlap, like bodies underground, and they become intimate in the strangest way.

When I first heard his voice it was like stones rattling in a pot. *You b-a-a-a-a-s-t-a-r-d*, he said. *I am not dead!*

It was not my voice in echo. It was something else.

He said, *Thank Christ you've quit ya screaming and carrying on. Between you and them fuckin' birds, a man gets no peace.*

The earth was moving around me like something was burrowing up. He pushed a small button through. He said, *Here, suck on this, kid.*

If I was at two feet, he was at three, and if my mother had kept on digging, she would have dug his bones right up. I took him at his word that it would have been a terrible sight to see. He said his jaw was blown clean off and that, over time, the worms had eaten him out completely. Of course, that's when he was still alive enough to be eaten. So physically, you would say, my companion was not much to speak of. It did not matter to me. I grew fond of him anyway, my neighbor at my elbow.

He became my measure of time. Every day, at the same hour that he was rolled into his grave forty years before, he yelled, *You bastard, I am not dead!* Every day it came out of him like an explosion and he said it was just his way of clearing the air. Apart from that, he did not say much. He said, *A lot o' fuckin' good words did me in life, so what good are they here?* But that did not stop sounds rolling out of him—rumbling and farting and moaning. He was never truly quiet.

And over time, he gave me more gifts. There was the button first, then came the spent bullet and a shell. I treasured each one. He also gave me an expression: *Bad to worse.*

He called me *kid.* I have said that he did not say much, but then one day, he did.

I heard him clear his gravelly throat and then he said, *Kid, sometimes a feeling can lurk around like a bad smell and after forty-odd years I'm thinking that a feeling must be better out than in. I dunno what it is, maybe it's listening to you, but I reckon there's something in the telling and you know I don't mind a few blue words and I'll keep it clean as I can, but you'll have to bear with me, kid.*

I've told you that my jaw was blown clean off and that's why my voice sounds like dry shit hitting a pot. Well, before I was buried, a bastard of a man took a piece o' my chin, just like he was biting into a bit of tough steak. I'm not one hundred percent a bastard—maybe just a bit—and I would have done the same, kid. I was stomping in his paddock where I shouldn't have went. You know what I mean, kid? I mean I had his wife.

So my arse was in the air and he was at the bedroom door and I only knew it 'cause I saw her face and her face told it all. But then her face changed as sudden as that and she lay there ginger as a cat, as if she wasn't guilty and we weren't stark naked in her old man's bed. I tore off the bedclothes, tried to wrap 'em around me, and leapt like a skinned rabbit from that bed, and then her husband smashed my shins with a chair. I fell down onto him so we were in a knot on the floor and I'd lost the sheet by then and my balls were dangling in the air—and I tell you there is no more dangerous feeling—and then the bastard kicked me right there and I wasn't seeing stars, kid, I was seeing planets and I just launched into him and I found his ear, and I bit a piece of it off.

I knew I had the smell of his woman on me, so I grabbed his hair and pressed my face into his so we were nose to nose and I said, Man, your woman tasted good!

That was something I shouldn't have said, kid. 'Cause that sent him wild. He locked his teeth around my chin and shook his head like a feral dog and then he spat me out and turned me over and jumped on the back of my legs and he jumped and jumped until he'd broken both my knees. And then he dragged me across that floor and I set my nails right in and clung to the very splinters but he dragged me anyway.

I blacked out then.

And this is the thing: I saw it, kid. It was my own imminent death. It was swift and it was sharp and it was dark and it was complete.

I came to as they loaded me in their cart. They were as silent as bastards and I couldn't see their faces, just the mean cones of their heads, the two of them. Any decent man would have left it at that. He'd broken my knees and crushed my balls. He'd defended his turf well enough. I would have just rolled out of there and dragged myself away and licked *my wounds and learned my lesson and not gone back to another man's wife. But no. This fella was a prick.*

They tied me up and drove me all night in their clapped-out wagon and I dunno why they chose this noisy spot, but they dug my grave right here and as some kind of punishment he had her sit on top of me so I wouldn't move and then when he was done digging, he handed her a gun and he said, Shoot him in the temple, love. She said, I can't, I can't. But she aimed at my temple anyway. I tell you, that woman was a cat. And would that she had done it right, kid, but she almost clean missed my head and that may have been my second chance at life but she didn't miss me clean enough and she blew off part of my jaw instead.

And she held the gun and seemed to tremble there for a while in shock until the man said, You're not to waste another bullet on that piece of shit.

That's when I started screaming, kid. I said, You bastard! Finish me off. I am not fuckin' dead!

Would that he had finished me off, kid, so I wouldn't be telling this story today or lying here haunted by what it was I saw when that bastard dragged me across his splintered floor. I know it was my own death that I saw, kid, like you know anything for sure. It was a good clean death. Not this drawn-out shit.

So how did I miss my chance at death, kid? Where's my good clean death after all?

Jack Brown lay on the bed in the station hut. There was a bare mattress beneath him and it sank with his weight. He told himself the cell was just like any other room, except for the bars across the windows. He had improved it by turning the lantern right down to a trembling flame, so he could not see the stains on the walls, and he had propped a chair against the metal door, just in case the wind got behind it and locked him in.

On the bed, he emptied out his pockets and found the postmaster's map. It was folded up and raggedy and softened by his own sweat. He drew up his knees and smoothed out the map and noted how many huts they had visited on the northwest arc.

To Jack Brown, each hut had been no more than a self-appointed cell and within them were lonely men whose very faces reminded him of what life could look like without tenderness, without a woman.

Riding from hut to hut, across country that was so familiar, Jessie was everywhere he looked. In each open paddock he could see some version of her rounding up cattle or showing off or making him laugh with some dirty tale she had heard in prison. But then, hut to hut, he felt the conflict within him, a steel trap in his chest that could lock him in its teeth at any minute.

Why had she deceived him?

He knew that in escaping, Jessie had escaped him, too. She had broken their pact of waiting. But then the sharp feeling that she had deserted him and left him to take the rap for her crime was matched by another. He wanted, again, to be riding beside her.

He needed to find the truth in it. That would be his only freedom. What seemed clear to him now was that it was not fate—that escaping together was just a fantasy and in reality he had only himself. The only way to find relief from fantasy or disappointment was to forget her, to strike off each memory like he was striking off each pencil-drawn hut from the map.

But how did he do that, when his memories of her were inked all over the landscape itself?

That night Jack Brown did not dream of my mother. He dreamt of Fitz. In the dream he and Barlow were not cutting the bellowing cow out of the barbed wire, they were cutting out Fitz. In the dream it was Fitz they freed. It was Fitz they watched run limping into the forest.

WHEN JACK BROWN WOKE in the morning he smelt himself and he smelt rank. He found his way to the washroom but he did not like the look of it, the broken mirror, the narrow tub, so he went outside and stripped down in front of the water tank. He splashed water over his body, soaped himself up and rinsed the soap off. He wiped off the water with his hands and he felt his skin finally alive with the heat of the sun.

Back in the cell, he dressed in fresh clothes, then he moved to the front of the hut, where he found Barlow sitting at the table, lamps and candles burning around him. His hair stood straight up in a greasy pile and there was ink all over his hands, his arms and his face.

Rough night? said Jack Brown.

Barlow held up his stained fingers in a salute and, without looking at Jack Brown, continued to roll ink onto plates of glass and press his fingers into them. Already there were pages of prints scattered across the table and across the floor.

It's all coming to the surface, Jack Brown.

Jack Brown's guts began to churn. He feared that after all these days of riding that Barlow was finally going to declare him as a suspect and arrest him.

Look here, said Barlow. *Look at this rise. Do you know there's not another man alive with fingerprints like them?*

Jack Brown looked at the prints and the lines and curves of them.

Press your finger onto the page.

Jack Brown froze up.

What are you afraid of?

Jack Brown pushed his thumb into the ink and then down onto the page.

It's just a smudge, said Barlow. *What are you, some kind of spirit child?*

Jack Brown looked at his thumb. The skin was marbled with ink. *Pulled too many pots from the fire, Sergeant.*

He was relieved when Barlow said, *I need you to hook those thumbs around your horse's reins. I need you to return to the postmaster's hut and pick up a delivery and I need you to do it soon.*

Jack Brown was happy to get out of there.

He mounted his horse and set off down Old Road. Riding, he could see the earth had begun to separate. Fine cracks revealed themselves across the surface of the road and riding over it was like riding over a patchwork of seams. At the edge of the road, the paddock was golden. He pushed out into it and the grass gave off a clean, fresh smell of heat and spring.

He rode on.

The mountains unfolded and soon he felt with all of his wanting that my mother would split the summit, come tearing out through the trees and ride determinedly towards him. But she did not.

Riding further into the day he thought he could make her out just ahead of him, and pelted towards her until he realized it was another trick of light and heat and nature.

Sometimes a path seemed to appear and Jessie could not tell if it was just a depression in the earth or if other men had walked upon it and walked it down. There were spurs and ridges that could send her off on the wrong course and some paths were split in four directions or more so that choosing a path seemed to be a test in itself: at the end of each path there would be a certain fate, waiting.

When Jessie did not have the assurance of the sun or the flowers with their sun-pointed heads to navigate by, she camped and waited for night. In the mountains a cloudy day often gave way to a clear night sky and she could always find within it the Southern Cross and below it the first bright star and she knew that south lay halfway between the foot of the Cross and the bright star, or the distance of her hands outstretched.

Jack Brown had taught her that.

Jack Brown did not ride straight to the postmaster's hut. He found himself swinging back towards Fitz's forest and soon enough he was pushing through its tangle of trees. And then when the scrub was too thick, he tied up his horse and walked through it.

He sat opposite his tree for a while and considered that facing what remained of Fitz might grow something mad in him, something beyond redemption, but then he thought redemption was just another false promise and he found himself prizing back the bark with his knife and pushing his fingers behind it.

A stench seeped out and Jack Brown stepped back and covered his face with his arm. He collected a stick from the ground and prodded the shield of bark from a distance.

The sack was in the tree, just as he had left it. Jack Brown took a deep breath, reached in and dragged it out.

It was mottled with damp and mold and there was a bright orange fungus growing up the side of it. He tested it with the stick and the stick sank right into it. He untied the rope and looked inside.

Fitz had lost all form, more swamp than human. For Jack Brown, these were hardly the remains that he had found in the cellar, that he had dragged and stuffed into the tree. This was something else, something that looked like it was dissolving in front of him. Here was some other warped version of nature, disintegrating beyond the normal flow of time.

Jack Brown tied the sack up again. He found a stronger branch and secured the sack to the branch with rope. Then he took off his boots and, holding the other end of the branch so the putrid bundle was well away from him, walked silently towards the river and there he filled the sack with stones, climbed upon a ledge and threw it in.

*B*arlow's back was killing him.

Alone at the station hut, he could find nothing to take his mind off the pain of it. He had riffled through Jessie's file so many times and he was too distracted to read his periodicals or his books on science. No theorem would numb him. He needed to fix on something tangible, something precise.

He began again to prepare glass plates and roll ink across them. He pressed his fingers onto the plates one by one and stamped them across a clean page as if somehow the repetition of the task might distract him from himself. Then he held them up, compared them again to Jessie's. They were not so different. Fingerprint to fingerprint, she did not seem so far. It was proof to him that she was at last within reach, that he would find her. But not on his own. He needed Jack Brown.

He pressed his fingers onto the page and then he smeared them across it. At last he heard Jack Brown traveling up the rise, the steady rhythm of his horse, the stretching of stirrups as he dismounted. Jack Brown would have his parcel and, as sure as science, soon there would be some relief from it all, soon everything would be all right.

But it was not Jack Brown. It was just a creature moving outside.

The pain in Barlow's back increased with his waiting. He lay across the table over the smudged and inky pages, weighting his body with his hips, hanging from the edge of it. He swung his hands above his head, swept his fingers over the floor until he felt the stretch in his spine, the traction of his body.

It brought him no relief.

He drank whiskey until he could not walk, he could only crawl. Later he crawled out of the hut and lay on the grass, waiting for Jack Brown. For a moment he felt the life in the stars charging him, sparking him at points, heat and light rushing across his chest, his knees, his groin.

He watched the stars shift against one another and his theorems collapsed together in his mind and he felt the force of himself to be insignificant, and inside or outside himself there was no equilibrium to find.

He fell asleep on the grass in front of the hut and he only woke when frost settled upon him like a glassy sheet.

J essie followed a northbound seam to its natural end and its natural end was a boulder. It was clear, just from looking, that Houdini could not pass between the boulder and the cliff face or the drop. And they could not turn back to wind down the narrow ledge they had already walked unless she was intent on suicide or being caught. It was easier, always, to climb with a horse.

Jessie patted Houdini's nose and left him licking the moss that covered the edges of rocks. She slid herself between the boulder and the cliff face to see what path lay beyond it.

As she moved herself around it, she could see a wider path opened up, at least half the size again of the path they were on. She wedged herself between boulder and cliff and, pressing her back against the boulder and pushing with her legs, she tried to force the boulder into the drop. But there was no moving it. Not even an inch.

She launched herself down and if it hadn't been for the wider path she might have tripped down into the drop for what she saw. Was it a joke? And whose joke was it?

A skeleton rested up against the boulder.

The bones of it were sun bleached and it rested against swirls of quartz and mica. A hat was tied under its chin and it was in one piece, more or less, aided by the weeds tangled through it.

Jessie took the skeleton to be a man and a man a long time dead.

She squatted down and rearranged his hat on his head. *Are you an omen?* she said. *Are you signaling that death lies ahead?*

Yet hatted and sun-bleached he did not look ominous but rather a comical thing, a friendly and mute guardian of a world beyond a world.

IF HE COULD HAVE SPOKEN BACK to my mother, he would have revealed that he had sat down in tiredness and in hunger. He had not wanted to serve in any man's war and he had escaped to the mountains for fear of conscription. He traveled up the rise, convinced he felt no shame in escaping. But then his shame finally expressed itself as he discovered he was unprepared for only the company of himself and he had no clue as to how to survive in the scrub and the wild of the mountain.

When he sat down against the boulder there was only enough breath in him to call out his own name, it was the only thing in his head. So that is what he did. And from where he sat, looking down into the saddle of the mountain, he heard his name called back. It came from a hundred different directions and although it satisfied him to hear—perhaps he would not be forgotten after all—it made him more disoriented than he already was.

He sat on the earth, but he could not get a sense of the earth beneath him. It was as if he were suspended and already floating down into the gaps of the mountain. He had grabbed at the tussocks of grass on either side of him and the torn-up grass with its dangling roots he took to be the finer threads of himself dislodged from the earth, life moving out of him.

He began to eat the grass as he had seen dogs do. He chewed and chewed and ground down the dirt and the grass and the roots with his teeth until there was only an oily cud in his mouth. He was conscious that whole day, turning the paste over in his mouth, until the heat struck from him the last of his life and a figure moved down the path towards him.

It was his final death. His short, sharp death in the form of his mother. Her arms were outstretched. She sang:

My darlin', sweet darlin', don't cry.
When the night spreads her blanket,
You'll sleep with the sky.

*T*he skeleton gave Jessie pause. She thought of what she could not bear to lose. With so much already lost she marveled that she could still feel it, the clinging feeling of what she could not be without.

Houdini.

She made a choice. If her own death was being flagged by the mountain, she did not want to take him with her. Houdini had life. He was escaping no one, so why should he be shackled to her fate?

She stroked his head and turned him back down the mountain. She hit his flanks.

Go, my friend, she said.

She watched him charge down the path.

Again, she climbed around the boulder, past the sitting skeleton. If her death was approaching, she would not grasp or fight as she had been fighting for most of her life. She would go willingly towards it.

She continued up the mountain.

She focused on the countryside and all that was outside herself. She fixed her eyes on all of its unfolding detail and marked that it was changing. Ribbon gum and brown barrel, hakea and grevillea grew wild against high basalt peaks that fell away to rugged rock-strewn slopes.

Each crevice seemed to hold within it a thousand varieties of life and as she walked along an escarpment and then a plateau she found herself within a labyrinth of rock, a watershed of country. She wondered why, if she had truly faced the certainty of her impending death and never again seeing Houdini, she still felt hope.

W hen Jack Brown returned to the station hut, Barlow looked to him to be in a trance. There seemed to be more paper strewn through the hut, though it appeared Barlow had not moved from the table since Jack Brown left.

Do you have it? said Barlow.

Jack Brown threw him his mail: a new issue of *Mind Power Plus* and a parcel wrapped in brown paper.

Don't throw it! said Barlow.

Jack Brown scratched his back against the edge of the doorframe. *Sergeant, it's already been shaken up all the way from Sydney.*

Barlow headed for the washroom with the packages tucked under his arm and Jack Brown heard him close the door behind him.

A man's business is his own, thought Jack Brown and he took his gun and moved outside again. The orange sky marked the end of the day and the bone-gray grass turned golden. He saw rabbits spring up between tussocks of grass. He perched his chin on the neck of the gun. Then, moving his eyes but not his arm, he fired a single shot.

His ears were still ringing as he moved down the slope, searching the grass until he found the rabbit. Its eyes were wide open. He twisted its neck to be sure it was dead and then he knelt down and skinned it. When the fur was clear of its carcass, Jack Brown opened it up and pulled out its intestines, its liver and the small green gland inside it. He dug a hole in the ground and buried the gland, as he knew it was poison. He tried to recall if he had removed it the last time he ate rabbit, but he could not remember. The task of catching a rabbit and skinning it was no longer a conscious thing. He had eaten so many of them.

Back in the hut he found a rusted pot in the kitchen and he scrubbed it with a metal brush and greased it with fat. He cut the rabbit into chunks and found an onion in the garden and a few potatoes and he sliced them up and set it all in the pot with water and salt. Breaking up sticks and twigs to fit in the belly of the stove, he made a dry bundle, lit it and blew until the chimney sucked up the flame. Fire crackled up against the iron, a sound that always made him feel good.

He had noticed nettles near the veranda and he knew they were good eating. He picked the spiky green leaves from their stems, then back in the kitchen, tore them up and added them to the pot. He stirred them in with the rabbit and watched their spikes folding down and softening and the water turn dark green as the stew started boiling up.

He knocked on the door of the washroom and said, *Sergeant, your dinner will soon be on the table.*

Jack Brown sat on the veranda and smoked cigarettes to quell his hunger. He smoked three, one after the other, but his hunger grew inside him anyway. While he was waiting he gave the horses new feed and cleaned out their yard. Then, when he was done, he went inside and tasted the stew. The meat was tender enough. He fried up the liver he had saved and when it was brown and bubbling at the edges he picked it from the pan with his fingers and ate it.

Barlow had not yet emerged from the washroom. Jack Brown knocked on the door and there was no answer. He yelled out, *You all right, man?* and Barlow shouted back, *Give me a call when my dinner is on the table.*

I'm not your black slave, yelled back Jack Brown.

What? said Barlow.

Your dinner is on the table.

Jack Brown cleared the long table that Barlow had layered with paper. He served the stew. Barlow appeared at the door looking as if he had not washed at all. He loitered for a while and then sat down.

Jack Brown ate hungrily and he thought the stew was good and thick with flavor. When he looked up, Barlow was staring at his fork and then his head fell forward and he jolted back up.

What's wrong with you, Sergeant?

I'm good, Jack Brown, I'm good.

Barlow started eating but mostly he moved things around on his plate.

Jack Brown went to the kitchen and filled his plate again. And he had finished off his second plate when Barlow declared that he was full enough and stood up, but instead of pushing his chair back he pushed the table forward and it hit Jack Brown squarely in the gut. Jack Brown thought his dinner would come up.

Barlow apologized over and over and offered Jack Brown a whiskey, which he declined.

Jack Brown had taken to smoking—it quelled a churning feeling—and he went outside and lit another cigarette. The night was still. Soon Barlow sat beside him with two heavy glasses and filled them right up and handed one of them to Jack Brown.

Sorry about that, Jack Brown—I lost my bearings.

Barlow sat on the edge of the veranda. He leaned against a post and kicked his boots out into the grass. There was a long silence between the men and it was so quiet that Jack Brown could hear the sound of Barlow swallowing.

Then Barlow said, *So what kind of man are you, Jack Brown?*

Jack Brown would have preferred the silence than to be asked that kind of question.

Do you mean am I queer? That kind of thing?

Barlow laughed. *I mean, a man can call himself many things.*

Like what? said Jack Brown.

Let's think about it. There's man about town, man of his time, said Barlow. His voice was drawn out.

What are you, Sergeant?

I don't know. I was hoping you might tell me. Barlow threw back his whiskey.

Jack Brown inhaled deeply and pointed to the constellations that were forming, but his mind was blank and he could not think of the names of any of them.

Do you think you can read people on sight? said Barlow. He poured himself another whiskey.

Do you mean if you can trust the man or not? said Jack Brown.

I've been reading about it in Mind Power Plus. *There's four types, it says. There's the Alimentative, the Muscular, the Osseous, the Cerebral.*

Jack Brown blew out a long stream of smoke. *I wouldn't be able to say if I was any of those, Sergeant*, he said.

Barlow brought his legs up to his chest and balanced his glass on his knee. He put his face behind it and examined Jack Brown through the amber liquid. *I'd say you were the Muscular type, Jack Brown. You know, all the great warriors were Muscular types.*

I'm no warrior, Sergeant, said Jack Brown.

The Muscular type, he's one for the open air, in constant motion, in accord with the laws of nature. That's gotta be you, Jack Brown. Barlow rested his head against the post and closed his eyes.

Jack Brown examined Barlow. There was a hopelessness about him, his limp hair flopping all over his face.

You need to sleep, Sergeant, said Jack Brown. *You look like a bit of a wreck.*

Barlow sat up. *You ever shoot up, Jack Brown?*

Rabbits. Roos. Cows, replied Jack Brown. *I shot at men in the war.*

Hats off to you, Jack Brown. But what I'm talking about is drugs. Have you shot any drugs into your veins?

No, Sergeant, said Jack Brown. *I've never had cause for that.*

Barlow staggered into the hut and returned with a small black leather case. He sat next to Jack Brown and made a performance of flicking it open by its silver tabs and unveiling its contents: a glass medicine bottle and parts of a syringe lodged between red velvet cushioning.

Heroin, said Barlow, holding up the small bottle.

What does it do for you? asked Jack Brown.

It's all in the name. It makes you feel like a hero.

A heroine is a woman.

Why don't you try it, Jack Brown? Decide for yourself.

Jack Brown crossed his legs and rolled another cigarette.

I'll go inside and fix it, said Barlow. He sprang up, seemingly suddenly energized, more energized than Jack Brown had ever seen him. He pulled a rubber cord from his pocket. *Tie this up below your elbow and pump your hand till you see your veins sticking out.*

Jack Brown rolled up his sleeves. The air was still and warm against his skin. The whiskey was taking effect, like a glow from his insides. He wondered what it would be like to feel like a hero or a heroine, on a calm night or any night, and then what did a man do when he felt himself to be one? Jack Brown wrapped the tourniquet around his arm and made a fist with his hand, as Barlow had instructed him to do. It felt good to do that and to see the dark, strong veins appearing under the surface of his skin.

When Barlow reappeared with two candles and a syringe between his teeth, Jack Brown's forearm was well lined with veins. Barlow sat down, placed the candles on either side of him and said, *Jack Brown, show me your muscles.* Jack Brown held out his arm and Barlow angled the needle into it. Barlow drew up the plunger of the syringe slightly. Jack Brown saw his own blood twisting inside it. He closed his eyes then, as Barlow pressed the plunger down and undid the tourniquet.

The tourniquet unfurled like a snake in Jack Brown's lap and he did not know what hit him. Heat teemed along his arm and moved up his neck and across his chest and down again. He leaned down, put his head between his knees, though the earth seemed to come straight to him.

The night wrapped around the hill and the sky pulsed with stars and planets. Jack Brown opened his eyes and felt his arms pinned down. He drew on all his strength to lift them. It was as if he was lifting weights. He managed to raise them up over his face so he could count ten fingers, which reassured him. He pulled himself back onto the veranda and swung himself around so his head hung off the end of it. He tried to determine which way was up and which way was down and then he searched for south by holding up his hands to the sky and by the angle of the stars, he knew where to find it.

As true as a compass.

And then he did not doubt where he was or why he was there. There were a thousand stars that he could not name and they were just a thousand versions of himself that he did not know and he felt no resistance, just degrees of goodness and badness all seeking each other, all wanting, somehow, to come together.

It did not matter then what he had done or not done. Around him the air was liquid and warm and he could move through it any way he chose. He sat up and he saw everything around him—the hut, the grass, the trees, the dark. They all drew in breath when he drew in breath and when he held his breath so did they all.

There was no distance then and no time. There were selves within selves enfolding each other. He had as much strength as the tree and as much force as the mountain. He was all the elements. He was the weather. It belonged to him.

He heard music then, and he did not know where it came from. He followed the sound and soon he found Barlow standing on the side of the hill playing a violin. The strands of his bow were snapping and flying around him.

The music moved into Jack Brown, right into the center of him, and he was possessed to drop to the ground on all fours. He felt in himself the spirit of the rabbit he had killed for their dinner and he leapt between tussocks of grass and was drawn on and on around the hill by the amber pools of light that appeared in front of him. He stood up then and felt himself to be a man complete, and around him was all of nature and he was nature's offspring.

The music stopped and the silence was sudden and serious. He sat on the ground. His legs looked to him like fallen trunks and he felt the curve of the earth beneath him. He craned his neck to the part of the sky directly above him and a tear rolled down his cheek. He did not feel it coming but he caught it on the end of his finger and raised it to the sky like some offering. In it he could see prisms of light and there were prisms opening all around him.

He stood up and looked for Barlow. He could see him on the top of the hill and began to walk towards him. He held up his arms to wave to him and Barlow began to yell. The sound coming from him was warped, like he was speaking underwater. Jack Brown walked closer. And then he heard him.

Where are the fucking women? he yelled. *Jack Brown, where are the fucking women?*

Jack Brown knew where the women were, he knew where to find them, and soon they were riding their horses unsaddled towards them. When they reached the end of Old Road, Jack Brown could not even remember calling the horses or mounting them.

You are a fucking hero, Jack Brown, shrieked Barlow as he galloped past him.

A wake of air folded around Jack Brown and he pushed his own horse into an echoing gallop. He heard it then, the earth disturbed and compacting as they rode, all of untold time beneath them.

fter three days of walking, Jessie could find no more water. The labyrinth of rock had given way to thick scrub that cut her as she walked. Her skin itched as though she had been bitten by thousands of insects. Lumps appeared on her hands and her feet, blisters upon blisters. If she'd had a needle or some sterile thing, she would have pierced them, neatly and one by one, and let the fluid drain out of them. But she did not have a needle. She leant against the rock face in the full sun and, starting with her hands, ran her jagged nail under the blisters and broke the skin and watched the claggy liquid inside them ooze out. She could not allow her feet to become infected but the blisters hurt to walk upon so she broke them, too. She began walking. The broken skin drew dirt to it but there was nothing she could do. She could not wear her boots. They had become containers for food and now they were too small for her swollen feet anyway.

She marveled that there was any excess moisture in her body, any water to spare, water enough to swell her feet or rise in blisters.

She found shade.

Her hunger was gone but her thirst was everything. She picked out the berries from her boot. They stung against the cracked skin of her lips so she tried to place the berries on her tongue although it hurt to open her mouth wider. She chewed and chewed them to create moisture.

All of it felt like waiting and there was no clear path to take and she missed her companion. The sun was disorienting and took up all of the sky and the bush was growing denser the higher she climbed. But still she was lucid enough to know the danger of her own thirst and that all day she had been stumbling. The ground beneath her was not a steady thing. Each step was uncertain and her feet seemed to sink through layers of dirt. She wished that days before she had filled her boots with water.

She walked on, barefoot, her gun strapped to her back, her boots hanging around her neck from their laces.

When she discovered footprints, she doubted what she saw. She thought at first that she was tracking herself, but then she measured them against her own foot and discovered they were not the same print, they were smaller.

She followed the footprints until she reached a plateau and then she saw that the plateau opened out to a clearing. She crouched low in the bush and searched beyond it. She could make out a holding yard. It was made of cut branches woven together in a circle, designed to keep horses and cattle, but she could see no creature in it.

She heard a whistling sound and she flattened herself under the bush. Looking out again, she saw a dog.

She moved along the ground as she had seen snakes and goannas do in the mountains, and hid herself behind a tree. She peered out. A boy was standing in the clearing. He was just a child standing there next to his dog. The dog's ears pricked up. The boy said, *What is it, Ned? What is it?*

The dog was still growling and edging closer to where Jessie hid but the boy was standing firm in the clearing.

Go get it, Ned—go get it!

And when she saw the dog come running in her direction she stepped out and yelled, *Down, Ned, sit down!*

Who's there? said the boy.

The dog was still barking so she stepped out into the clearing. The boy moved closer and raised his gun and she said, *Don't shoot me, kid.*

Who are you? he said.

My name is Jessie.

The boy stood with his gun pointing at her and the dog ran to his side.

Put your gun down.

It was weeks or more since she had seen another human and so much longer since she had seen a boy. They regarded each other and she could see the beauty of his form, as elegant as anything she had ever seen, mountain, river, rampart or tree. And as the boy and the dog stood visibly disbelieving what they were seeing—*a woman*—she wondered as she approached if beauty was just the thing itself or made more beautiful by the space around it.

Fucking Jesus, Ned. It's some kind of woman.

Mind your tongue, she said, and laughed. As if she was one to say that.

Sorry, miss, said the boy, and then the dog started barking and began to bark in a frenzy and the boy knelt down beside him and rubbed him under the chin, which made the dog quiet.

Kneeling there he said, *What brings you to here?*

She knelt down, too, and didn't think much of it and just said, *The same things, I expect, that brought you.*

The boy led her to his camp, which was near a waterhole, and it was the best camp she had ever seen. There were rocks there and boulders that formed like honeycomb and grottoes big enough to stand in. She could see that some of them were already lined with bedding and there were branches wedged into corners with things hanging from them—clothes and bridles and coats.

There are five more of us here, said the boy, *but they are not here now. They are all off selling horses. And, miss, it is better that you don't tell anyone that we are here or not here because we like things as they are and you are the first to have found us. We have all that we need here and there'll be more when they get back, you'll see, 'cause they'll bring supplies. There'll be johnnycakes with golden syrup and Bill cooks things the best on the fire, like pumpkin and roo and fish from the creek. And when they come back they'll bring more oranges, too, and limes, 'cause Joe says if we don't eat 'em our teeth'll fall out—and Joe says that there are no tooth fairies here, we do not believe in 'em. Who would? And we've made a garden, too, but that's on the other side of the creek, 'cause it was bringing in too many roos and creatures on this side. More than we would want to eat or kill, miss. More than we would want to eat or kill.*

They made a fire together that night. The boy gave her an orange and it was lit up by the fire like the brightest orb and he said, *There are only two left but they will be back soon and there will be more.* She shared the orange with the boy and it was the best she had ever tasted. The dog sat between them and he had calmed right down but lifted his head up occasionally and looked at her and then his head sank down meekly on his paws. *Don't mind Ned, miss. He's never seen a woman who is grown.* And she laughed because although she was a woman who was grown she felt no different to the boy or to how the boy must have felt—happy to have found someone to share an orange and a fire at the summit of the mountain.

They gazed at the fire and they saw all things in it, creatures of the earth and creatures of the air, and they took turns at naming what they saw or guessing what hybrid that creature could be.

The sky was vast and clear and hung above them, revealing stories in its constellations for anyone who looked. And as the fire dwindled they did look up and they recognized some of its stories and some they did not know but told anyway, making the stars their own. It was the roof of their world and they were at ease with their world, looking up and feeling that they had explored great distances in the universe that night, all the while sitting by the dwindling fire.

They saw a girl spinning. Her hair was like a comet's tail, splitting against the sky. And when they blinked they could both see the thousand smaller stars that made the detail of her collar and a thousand more that made the buttons and seams from her wrists to her elbows. Hair and lace collars and buttons all made of stars.

As the girl was spinning, a Master of Menace bore down from the west, and his cape was made of darkness, not of stars. He threw back his cape and from his boots he drew a knife and launched it through the night, aiming at the girl who was still spinning.

And then out of the night a lasso fell around him and the girl got away and circled her opponent on her dappled horse. She circled him and then she did a handstand and the boy and Jessie saw all of this playing across the sky until they finally lost her when she flipped off her horse and tore out of their view.

What did you do down there, miss, with all of your days?

Rustled horses and cattle mainly.

Rustlin'—you mean stealin'?

Plain and simple. Horses and cattle, both. We'd bring them in, rebrand them and sell them on the other side of the mountains.

I'll be sure to tell Joe that, said the boy.

And then he said, *You know we're a gang, miss. Me and Joe and the others. And you been rustlin'. I'll be sure to tell Joe.*

The boy nestled his head into Ned's rump and his arm fell across the length of the dog's long body.

Don't mind us, Miss Jessie, said the boy, his words running together in his tiredness. *Ned and I sleep out like this all the time.* The boy and the dog then closed their eyes in unison.

Jessie fed more wood into the fire and arranged herself on the other side of it. By the time she lay down the boy was sleeping, his head rising and falling with the breathing of the dog.

She rolled onto her side and put her hand under her temple, as a pillow. But she did not close her eyes. She could not take her eyes off him.

*D*ays and days passed and the boy kept saying, *They'll be back soon, miss, they'll be back*. All of his talking was like a mad little tick and she began to worry for them, Joe, Bill and the others. She imagined them, hungry as thieves.

Jessie and the boy set themselves jobs to keep their minds off the others' absence. They tidied the camp and chopped wood. They waded across the waterhole to the green garden, where everything grew beautifully in rows—spinach and lettuce and rhubarb, and pumpkin vines that had been cordoned off with string. The whole thing was fenced off with pieces of chicken wire tied together with twine. Attached to sticks stuck into the ground were tins made into propellers that whirred in the wind. *We made them to keep the birds away*, said the boy. She asked the boy whose idea it was to grow their food and he said, *That was Joe. He is the oldest one here. He is sixteen*.

More days passed and Jessie began to wonder if it was just going to be her and the boy and the dog forever, and if something had happened to the rest of them. And she worried more for them when she turned her mind to all the things that can happen droving horses and selling them. She did not tell the boy her concerns. But by the way he was fidgeting, she guessed he was thinking the same thing.

It was half dark when she was woken by a vibration in the earth like an earth tremor and it soon heralded a great cavalcade of horses and then the sighs of their riders dismounting.

She watched them from her bed, which was a cave in the rock, and she could see the riders all drawing nearer the fire, where the boy was waiting. She could see from their silhouettes that all of them were lean and some of them were as tall as saplings, and they all stood gently together, and they all leaned down to embrace the boy. Then the one she took to be Joe lifted the boy onto his back and jigged him around the fire until they were all laughing.

When she rose the sun was high in the sky and the boy was up and he was unloading supplies into the camp kitchen, which was another cave with its opening on the ground. The cave was deep enough to stand up in and the gang had built shelves, balancing them on rocks and sticks, and on the shelves were cans of things and things in sacks. Hessian bags covered the opening of the cave and some of them were rolled up and tied and the boy passed supplies under to someone on the other side.

The boy said, *Jessie, this is Bill. Bill is the best cook on the mountain.*

Bill was standing behind the makeshift curtains and he opened them gingerly. *Hello, Jessie,* he said. His voice was strangely deep. He had a mop of black hair, eyelashes that swept his cheekbones when he blinked, and dark, golden skin. From his eyes and his skin, Jessie guessed he was Aboriginal. She offered her hand and he shook it back but there was no doubt that behind those lashes he was regarding her with suspicion.

Jessie wandered around the camp and saw signs of its inhabitants that were not there before. Boots kicked off outside the caves, saddles propped up off the ground and ropes in circles in the dirt. And then walking into the clearing she saw that while Joe and the others may have sold horses they had brought back a dozen more. The horses in the holding yard were wild; kicking and bucking and biting, they were trying to establish who ruled in the yard and beyond. She observed them all with a distant curiosity, wild creatures fighting, until she saw what she wished she would see. Houdini was in there among them, more ragged than she had last seen him, but still rearing up like any belligerent stallion.

There was no way out for any of the horses. The branches were piled high and made sharp at the ends. Jumping would mean breaking their neck or their legs in the tangle of sticks. She couldn't bear to see Houdini in there, scraping around wild and fighting with the others. Keeping her head down, she let herself in through the thatched gate. Houdini saw her, made a path to her, and then they walked a lap of the yard, around its edge, to calm the chaos of the others. When she neared the gate again, Jessie opened it quickly and together they slipped out.

There was a wooden box near the holding yard with leather straps for hinges and when she opened it up she found what she needed—brushes, bridles, ropes and leads. While Houdini pushed his nose into her neck she chose a brush. And then she led him to the shade of a tree, away from the holding yard and the brimming discontent of the other horses, and she brushed him down.

Under his coat patches of skin had been torn and healed rough and other patches were covered with burrs. His mane was matted into cocoons and within them were live colonies of insects. She clipped them out and brushed him down and he stood as still and content as she had ever seen him.

She was about to swing herself up onto him to ride him through the bush when the boy appeared and behind him Bill and an older boy she took to be Joe.

And it was Joe who said, *Well, what have we here? Who's this who has found us and now rides our horses?* He was smiling, though, and his eyes were kind and bright.

This is Houdini, my horse, and I am relieved to find him. I had to leave him to his own devices or we would not have made it up the mountain, him or me.

How do we know it is your horse? said Bill, whose voice now was high-pitched and nervous.

Well, he let me lead him out of that ruckus and brush him down and soon you will see me ride him.

The boy was turning stones over with the toe of his boot and Joe and Bill looked so serious standing there.

We'll need to consult with the others, said Joe, *about if you can stay.*

I had not thought of it, said Jessie. *The boy and I discovered each other and we have been good company but now that you are here and I have my horse, it may be best to leave.*

We'll talk on it with the others, said Joe. Jessie nodded without speaking, then Joe added, *You see, you are the first to have found us and the boy tells me you can rustle. As you may have guessed it, that is what we do, and though we're not recruiting it seems that you've traveled a long way—it's a long way up, we know. It seems that it is some kind of coincidence that you have found us, though we do not yet know where that coincidence might lead to. But give us the day to talk it over and we'll make a decision about what we should do.*

Jessie nodded again and swung up onto Houdini's back and rode him slowly out of the clearing. The boy came running after her. He'd wrapped up half a fresh damper in a bit of cloth.

This is for your lunch, he said. *But come back before dark.*

It was still early morning.

I'll be back, she said. *Don't worry about that.* And she winked at him and turned Houdini towards the scrub. When she looked back, the boy was still standing there, watching.

For so long, she had wanted to be in the mountains. She had thought only of escape. She had dreamt of her freedom and now that she had it, she did not know what to do with it. She led Houdini along a ravine and then she sat by it, as if the ravine itself would speak up and offer her counsel.

She ate the damper the boy had given her, then she lay down on her back and watched the clouds passing over. There were forms racing cloud to cloud and she could see creatures in those forms and creatures becoming other creatures, each thing changing and nothing ever visible for long. And it was all set against the pristine sky and it was all moved along by the wind.

Houdini tore at the grass with his teeth and the sound of it was music to her ears. She lay there with Houdini beside her until the clouds became like wool, all spindling over.

She thought of the boy. The boy reminded her of Bandy Arrow. Yet she knew that no matter how much time she spent around the fire with the boy, it was not a story she would share.

It had been thirteen years since she had last seen Bandy Arrow, and the last time she had seen him was the fall. It remained so clear to her, the sounds and textures of it, and she wondered how that memory, after all these years, could still carry such feeling.

The night of his fall, she was standing on the balustrade, urging him forward. On the tightrope he was as light as a feather and his balance was perfect, and yet he was afraid of heights. She had climbed the ladder with him, as she did every night, and every night she said to him, *Bandy, don't look down.* There was no safety net at Mingling Bros. Circus and that was what set the circus apart—the danger was real. From the balustrade, she would concentrate on his feet and will him safely, step by step, across the rope. Mirkus called the two of them "the winning combination"; with Jessie's help, Bandy had performed the stunt successfully every night for a year. But this night, for some reason, he looked down.

To her eyes, his feet were not the first things to slip. It was his body that shifted away from the rope and he fell sideways and then down. He landed feetfirst. There were screams from the crowd and then gasps of awe as some of them thought for a moment they were witnessing something miraculous, a freak performer. But when he hit the ground he kept on traveling, his spine on a vertical path downwards, his legs redirected. The incompatible destinations were measured at his knees and like a hinge without a spring he collapsed.

She rushed down the ladder and to his side along with Mirkus, the ringmaster. And she had cried as she held Bandy's head and turned it to the side while he vomited out the shock he was in.

It's nobody's fault, said Mirkus. *Sometimes we just fall.*

He called for a stretcher and Bandy Arrow was loaded onto it and carried away. Jessie went to follow but Maximus said, *We must keep performing, that's all we can do.*

And so she did.

And when the show was over and the crowd shuffled out, she returned to the place where he had landed. There were strokes in the dust where his fingers had made trails and his limbs fanned out.

She traced his imprint on the ground. That was it. She knew she would not see Bandy Arrow again.

WHEN SHE WOKE it was almost dark. Houdini was standing, a towering creature, nudging her arm with his nose. She sat upright. She felt odd—as if some great fissure had finally opened up, and all of the convolutions of herself were meeting at the surface, like so many coincidences at once. And somewhere in it all was her own distinct nature.

Sitting by the ravine she felt her past was not behind her or beneath her, it was everywhere at once, living through her, and the boy and Joe and Bill were just like those she had known before and here on the mountain was something like a second chance, a chance to love well, and she did not yet know its limits.

When she returned to the camp, the gang was all sitting around the fire. She could see the boy and Joe and Bill and another three among them. Joe stood up and welcomed her and she sat down and they all smiled at her and she could smell sweet things roasting on the fire.

Joe remained standing. *The boy says you are a rustler. We know that you are brave enough to take on the mountains and walk through a yard of wild horses and lead your own horse out. And you know we have a gang and we aren't recruiting; we are solid as we are. But now that you are here, we believe there is some fate in it. You have seen that we bring in wild horses and some of them are branded and we sell them, and we sell cattle in the same way. And we prefer to live here, as we are, for now. We are safe from all that would harm us. But there may be a day when we have to move on and each of us will do that as they please. One day we may build a house of our own and all of us will live in it together. And there may be a time when we don't have to do things that are illegal. But that day has not come and until it does we'll keep on because we have all run from something one by one. Just as you have found us we have all found one another, like magnets attracting. And now we are happy that you are among us. And not to offend you, miss, but we guess you are older than us—old enough to sell our stock at the sale yards.*

Joe sat down and everything fell to silence. He was a natural leader and he took things seriously and he spoke with all sincerity. Joe looked to Bill and their eyes met and both were brightened by the flame. Jessie took in the other faces around the fire, all of them young and bright and shining, and they were all looking at her quietly, waiting for her to respond.

Joe, all of you, riding horses and stealing cattle is what I do, and I know I do it well. And it is my good fortune that I have found you. I have been in these mountains alone for too long, and without knowing it, it is your company that I have craved. I would like to be counted as one of you.

The next day Jessie was up before the rest of them, making a fire and tea. The air was damp that morning and the wood was slow to light and the camp looked like it was deposited not on a mountain but on a cloud. She sat cross-legged on the ground, feeding the fire with kindling and blowing on it to bring it to life.

Slowly the rest of them emerged from their caves. One by one they sauntered through the fog, their collars up and their shirttails out, their hair twisting in cowlicks around their foreheads and their crowns. Never in all of her life had Jessie seen more elegant or perfect creatures. They moved in towards the fire, quiet with the sleep that still hung about them. She ladled sweet tea into tin mugs and she took pleasure in watching them roll their faces over the steam.

The boy ran off and brought back a bag of oranges. He handed one to each of them and they all became animated, biting off the skin with their teeth and throwing the skin into the fire and laughing as the juice dripped down their chins. The air carried the companionable smells of tea and oranges and soon it was all mixed with the smell of oats cooking.

Jessie noticed Joe was drawing shapes and lines on the ground with a twig and she asked him, *Are you planning something?*

And one of them, Zef, who was missing a front tooth, added, *Is it almost time?*

In a week or so the moon will be new, said Joe. *Yes. It will soon be time to head back down to Phantom Ridge and bring in the cattle.*

There's still a week's work in the ropes and preparing, said Bill. *And we'll need everybody's hands if we are to get down there by the new moon as Joe plans.*

As they ate breakfast Joe explained the heist to Jessie.

Miss, we've been planning this six months and our thinking is that we will do but one big haul in a year and it will be enough for us to live well and buy all the supplies we need and it will give a healthy cut to all of us. There are five of us who can drive it, not including the boy, and now with you there are six and by our count there is almost a hundred head of cattle to move in the night. Soon the sky will be at its darkest and that is the best time for vanishing things, you know. The rope you will see will be like one giant lasso, only we will not throw it like that. We will herd the cattle together and we will keep the rope low around them and then we will move them. We will all have a hand in it. And of course there is risk, there always is, of stampede, but watch and see if the dark moon doesn't dull those beasts completely.

As Joe spoke the plan and continued to make marks on the ground, Jessie's heart raced inside her. It was so long since she had been droving. Fitz had put an end to it when he discovered she was pregnant when she was too large to hide it from him. Under Fitz's rule, droving and duffing were her only experience of freedom, however fleeting.

And when you move them, how will you get them to sale? she asked.

Wait till you see it, miss, said Joe. *Inside these mountains is a miracle. There's a whole system of caves and tunnels that runs from the north side to the south, and over time we have tracked and mapped our way through them and out to the other side. We'll have to get them to the sale yards in under two days, before the owner finds his cattle gone and before he can send warning. But in that time we can get them there if we move them day and night. We will stop only to rebrand them. Zef here has a calligrapher's hand and he has drawn us up a certificate, a note from the owner if you like, though it looks like a letter from the prime minister himself. "I hereby declare this is my cattle and I give these drovers full license to sell them on my behalf." And if you could tuck your hair up, miss, we have a few smothers that you can wear. If you don't mind me saying, you are handsome-like and you could pass easily for a gentleman. And between us we could represent the owner well.*

IT TOOK ALL OF THEM to spread out the ropes and when they were done the ropes looked like pale vines stretching through the camp. There were seven ropes in all and six joins that needed to be woven together. The gang took their places on the ground and set about weaving; Jessie watched on as the boy unplaited the two ends of rope and then, with practiced hands, began to weave them together. She watched intently the pattern of his interlacing fingers and then she asked him to slow down so she could learn the pattern herself, to relieve him. The boy then demonstrated the sequence by counting. It was elaborate to her eyes.

Why don't you tie them together? she asked, as she could begin to gauge just how long it would take to join them all.

A knot just wears down the rope, miss, said the boy. *And a weave is much stronger than a knot, you know—and after you and Joe and the others bring in the cattle we have other plans for this rope, miss, and it should remain a surprise to you but you will soon see that there should be no knots in it at all.*

Jessie watched the boy and the others and none of them seemed to fatigue of their work. She stretched out in the sun next to the boy and said, *Tell me when you're tired.*

And the boy said, *I will do, miss.*

She relaxed completely then in the uncommon peace she felt in their company.

By the end of the second day the six joins were made and there was one complete rope and they measured it in strides and made sure it met the dimensions they had measured first by horse length on their reconnaissance.

Joe explained to Jessie that although they had first conceived the rope working as a giant lasso their aim was not to close the rope around the cattle but more use it as a moving fence, taut, pushing the cattle from behind.

They practiced with the rope, looping sections of it over their arms and their shoulders and then spreading it out in one orchestrated movement around the campsite. The boy stood in the middle of their circle and signaled to them the proper timing of the rope's release. Aside from a few rope burns on their arms they deemed it a success.

The moon was soon dark and Jessie, Joe, Bill and the rest of the gang prepared to set off, leaving the boy and his dog behind. The boy's job was to guard the camp, though Jessie heard Joe tell him that if anyone approached the site he was to hide himself and his dog. *Take yourself to the cave on the other side of the waterhole,* he said, *and if we come back and you're not here, we'll know where to find you.*

They all took turns hugging the boy or roughing his hair before they mounted their horses and he walked them out to the ridgeline. His dog at his side, he waved them off as they stepped their horses down one by one. They moved cautiously along the narrow track; later, when the track allowed it, they rode side by side. There was an easy feeling among them and as they rode they practiced birdcalls and sometimes the birds seemed to call right back, as if they were all a part of some earthly communion whose only subject was beauty and gratitude.

Sometimes the slope was too steep to ride and they led their horses and walked them close along crumbling tracks. Soon they entered caves and tunnels so large they dwarfed their party of six plus the six horses.

After two days of riding, they reached the edge of the northern range. At Joe's instruction, they halted within a cave and painted the hooves of their horses white. They could not risk lighting fires so they passed the time eating their food raw and whispering their plan among them until it was dark.

When Joe said it was time, they each gathered a part of the rope and looped it around their arms and their shoulders and then they mounted their horses and Joe led them out. It was dark but for a sliver of moon and they could hardly see or be seen but Joe said, *Just keep your eyes on the horse's hooves in front of you.* And then when the paddocks opened up they formed a line and each of them tugged on the rope both ways to signal they were still connected to one another.

They heard the cattle first and proceeded towards the sound, keeping pace with one another, measuring their distance by the hooves that appeared as luminous streaks near the ground in front of them. When they were close to the herd, they unwound the rope from their arms and rode out in a curve, making no sound or signal other than what the tension of the rope revealed.

Riding in a circle, they drew the rope out around the cattle and moved them back towards the direction of the cave. The cattle moved slowly and there was no protest in them.

The gang moved the herd across the field and each cow was barely distinguishable, no more than bleached patches of night floating in some strange order.

It took them half the night to reach the cave. When they arrived at the mouth of it, they closed the rope in and funneled the cattle inside. Then it was Jessie and Bill's job to drove them up into the narrower passages, while the other four went back, in haste, to remove any evidence around the perimeter of the cave, which amounted to filling bags with dung that they scooped up with pieces of bark they carried with them.

When they reconvened they all herded the cattle through the tunnels and then cave to cave until they arrived at what they called Branding Point. It was a cave split at the top with a natural chimney that would let smoke out and it was far enough away from Phantom Ridge to remain unseen by anyone in the morning patrol of the cattle.

They had hidden lanterns and branding irons on previous missions and even experimented with fire beneath the split. They used the same pit to light a fire, and set the branding irons against the coals until they glowed purple. Then they took turns to hold and brand the cattle. Each creature shuffled its bulk and bellowed as they pressed the iron into its hide. But the cave was well chosen, a cave within a cave, and all sounds there were contained within the chambers of the rock.

When the cattle were all rebranded, they moved on. There were five lanterns among the gang and they lit them all, although it was not the dark that bothered them, more the asphyxiating smell of dung as the cows released more readily into the narrow passages of the cave.

By the next morning they had reached the southern side. They hid the rope and their lanterns within the cave and herded the cattle into the daylight, moving them steadily towards the sale yards. Joe and Jessie paused to tidy themselves. Bill had made mustaches for them by snipping pieces of their hair, weaving them onto small scraps of fabric and now pasting these onto their top lips with a mix of flour and water. Joe and Jessie looked at each other and laughed at what a handsome pair they made.

When they arrived at the sale yards, Joe and Jessie presented the clerk with the forged letter. The hand was elaborate and the paper was watermarked and the clerk had no reason to question it. A stockman inspected the cattle and then a sale in cash was made.

The gang breezed through the township as easily as any band of drovers and there was no evidence of what they had done, aside from the money in their pockets and the lingering smell of dung they carried in their nostrils.

They had vanished a hundred head of cattle.

They did not waste their time with town things but found a store and bought dried biscuits and sweet milk and new boots and shirts and a pulley, and in no time they were on course again, riding back in the direction from which they had come.

When they reached the opening to the cave they collected the rope and lanterns but did not continue farther in. They all needed air and country. It would take them a few more days but they were happy not to move into the tunnels until they were halfway up the mountain.

That night, they camped out in the open. In the morning, when Jessie woke, she could see horses grazing in the distance. They looked as though they were covered in frost, ghostly shapes all of them. She had an impulse to go after them, but she held herself back and just watched. One of the horses stirred and turned its long head in her direction as if it had suddenly become aware of her. Then it surged out and all of them disappeared into the denser mountain.

Jessie lay back, heard the thrumming of their hooves echoing down. She thought of Jack Brown. It came with a heavy feeling.

THERE WAS A WHOLE YEAR between the first time they were together and the second. And after the first time, she cold-shouldered him. They continued to ride together and drove, but she kept a great physical distance from him at all times. She believed that both their lives would be in danger if Fitz found out what had happened.

Over the years, she had done her best to ward off Fitz's advances. But sometimes she could not. He called it her *wifely duty.* Some nights she was saved because he was too drunk to scratch himself and for half the month she told him she was bleeding, which repulsed him so much he avoided her for another week again. So that left a week or a few days a month to evade him as best she could. She had learned from the women in prison how to synch her cycle with the moon and for years of managing this and Fitz she had never fallen pregnant.

She could think of no worse thing.

But then one morning she woke and Fitz was already on top of her. She knew it would be more punishing to resist him.

Four weeks later she suspected she was pregnant. Five weeks later she was certain.

It consumed her but she told no one. She even copped a beating from Fitz but still she kept it from him.

Six weeks later, she was droving with Jack Brown.

He was asleep in his swag and she went to him.

Kissed his neck.

She felt herself unfreezing.

He woke and he did not stop her.

In the morning he said, *What took you so long?*

And she did not check herself when she said, *Jack Brown, I do not want to die by Fitz's hand.*

They were gentle with each other all day and then their days of riding passed in a haze. Two months later, on another ride she told him, *Jack Brown, I am pregnant.*

Is it mine, he asked, *or is it Fitz's?*

I believe it's yours, she said.

With all her heart she wished me to be Jack Brown's child. But all of her wishing could not make it true. She had deceived him.

When the gang woke, they lit a small fire and made tea and dipped dried biscuits in sweet condensed milk. They saddled their own horses and rode them through the thick scrub in pairs. For sport, when they spotted a wild horse they would charge up behind it. If they could get close enough, one of them would grab its tail, which slowed it sufficiently for the other to make a short throw and slip a rope over its head. Then they would tie the brumby to the nearest tree until it had tired itself of kicking and bucking and then guide it on.

Jessie paired up with Bill. They rode in silence for most of the day and Jessie was grateful for it. The day was almost spent and they were riding close through thicker scrub when Bill said, *Miss, you may have guessed it, my name is not Bill—it is Layla, but no one here except Joe knows me as that.*

Layla is a girl's name, said Jessie.

Yes, miss.

You are a good rider, Layla, or Bill, whatever your name is.

Thank you, miss, but I've seen that none of us are as good as you.

That's just 'cause I've ridden longer.

They ducked beneath the trees. Jessie was curious about how Layla came to call herself Bill. *Where were you before you came here?* she asked.

Me and Joe were working up north on a station. I was working as hard as a man but sometimes even that is not enough. The station owner wanted me to herd his cattle by day and be his bed companion at night. But I did not want to, miss. And Joe was my friend, a real friend who looked out for me. We droved together and although he is not black, as you can see, he was young and neither of us was treated well there. And the station owner said that I must do as he said and he said that he owned me and I did not want to be owned. So I left with Joe, miss. We ran away.

Layla—Jessie began.

Please, miss, around the gang I want you to call me Bill.

That night the gang tied all the horses they had captured to trees and they camped on high and uneven ground. They sprawled out on their backs and Bill pointed out a constellation and she called it Pleiades. *All of them stars there are related. Can you see, miss, there are seven of them? One for each of us. They are almost blue and you will see that they are all moving in the same direction across the sky, all moving in a cluster. But we are a gang and all of those stars are sisters and they are being chased by one man. They are all running from him, but he will not catch them.*

Why not? said Jessie.

He cannot, miss. That man there, he is locked in the sky.

The next morning, they saw that more horses had gathered in around the ones they had caught. They did not have enough ropes to capture them but as they moved slowly back up the steep slope the horses followed and then, as if one of their gang had cracked a whip, all of the horses veered off at once, leaning their bodies sideways, far away and east of them.

V

October now. A month or more since she had gone and the only trace of the September winds and storms was a subdued whistling that came and went. Jack Brown's horse hustled back and forth and then there was just the tinkling of stirrups and buckles, the slapping of leather against flanks, and he would have preferred to be harbored by some din than to be alone with the sounds of himself, a horse, a gun.

He looked upon the great spread of the mountains. The blue mystery of their trace folded out into obscurity. It gave him no relief to contemplate them, knowing that she was there, somewhere within the trees, the long stretches of scrub, the larger forest.

Now, as always, she felt as impossible as a dream.

Even riding with her, through grove or open field, he always felt that she was already far away, moving on some different path. And many days he felt his own horse was made of clay and they were being towed in her wake and all he could do was hold on and do his best not to slow her as she lit out at breakneck speed. She rode like she would not stop till she reached the horizon and there was no telling where her horse ended and where she began.

Was it love, then, to want to capture her?

It did not feel right to him. But in truth he had wanted her to be his.

His horse shifted sideways and back in the field. He turned his shoulder against the mountains and his horse followed the lead of his turned body and they moved towards the station hut.

HE FOUND BARLOW crawling through the kitchen on his hands and knees. He had his nose right down to the floor like a dog. Jack Brown leaned against the doorframe and folded his arms. He watched Barlow following an ant trail that snaked across the kitchen floor, disappeared behind a cupboard and then reappeared on the wall. He watched the sergeant angle his thin arm around the back of the cupboard and press his face flat against it as he twisted half of his body around to retrieve the perfect skeleton of a bird. He wasn't talking to Jack Brown when he said, *Look at that!*

I am, said Jack Brown.

Barlow clutched the bird against his chest and drew up his knees like a chastised child. He stared up at Jack Brown, his eyes pulsing in his head.

Must have flown in and died, said Jack Brown.

The remains of the bird were strung together by ribbons of flesh that the ants were making short work of. Soon the ants were crawling all over Barlow and he brushed himself frantically with one hand, holding on to the bird with the other.

A pounding on the station door startled them both.

Jack Brown was immune to Barlow's antics now, so an unexpected visitor to the police hut was more bizarre than the scene in front of him.

Do not make a sound, said Jack Brown, and he left Barlow squeezing himself between the cupboards.

Jack Brown opened the front door in time to see the wide back of a man heading around the side of the hut.

Hey! said Jack Brown. *What's your business here?*

The man turned around to face him. His face was typical of most faces Jack Brown had seen in the valley. A face as sunburnt and soiled as old leather.

So someone's manning this hole after all. I was about to give up when I saw those horses in the yard and I thought nobody would be stupid enough to leave horses like that. Not even a city copper. Or his black tracker.

Word travels fast. How can I help you, sir?

Get me your big-city sergeant.

He's not here.

I'll wait.

Fair enough, just take a pew and we'll see if he's back by tomorrow morning.

The man sat down and surveyed the view from the hill.

And who are you anyway? asked the man.

Jack Brown. But you can call me the black tracker.

Expected you'd be blacker. Jack Brown, eh? I'm a cattleman. And one hundred head of my cattle has gone missing. The man clicked his fingers. *Jack Brown, my cattle just fucking gone!*

Any idea who did it?

The man dragged his feet in and sat forward. *Truth is, it could have been any one of the desperate bastards around here. But one hundred—that's a real job. Those bastards usually just skim, like cream off the milk. But one hundred. Jack Brown, that's the milk and the cream.*

One hundred.

A real fucking vanishing act.

Where's your land?

Up there. He pointed to the far mountains. *Near Phantom Ridge. Sidling up the north end.*

Jack Brown knew it. A stretch of land against the northern band of the mountains. He had ridden through it with Jessie and they had skimmed some of the cattle for themselves.

How many days they been missing?

Five days or so. I've been out looking for signs of them myself. You'd think that one hundred head of cattle, they'd leave some trail. But this is the thing, Jack Brown—I couldn't even find a trace of their shit. The man scratched his beard with his blunt fingers. *Not even a trace of shit.*

The man stood up. *I got no time to waste, Jack Brown. Get some of your black-fella magic on to it. When cattle goes missing without a trace, it makes for a very uneasy feeling around here. There are ex-soldiers all over holed up in their huts. They're all guarding their shitty bit of land and a couple of skinny cows. They're already spooked. They get word of this, a hundred head just vanished, and they'll be out with their guns shooting at the fucking dark, wanting a bit of it themselves. They'll be racing around like fucking lame vigilantes.*

The man walked along the veranda. Jack Brown followed him and watched him mount his horse.

We'll need someone to blame for this, Jack Brown, and I hear from good sources that an ex-convict woman is loose and she is famous for her rustling.

I haven't heard that, said Jack Brown. *And surely you can't pin a hundred cattle on one woman.*

Rumor is she killed her husband, too. Two birds with one stone, Jack Brown.

I'll report it to the sergeant.

You know, said the man, *in the dark a copper and his tracker look the same as any other woman or any other man.*

Is that a threat, sir?

The man turned his horse. *We're still old-fashioned out here, Jack Brown. We like someone to blame.*

The man took the reins out wide and then he rode away. Jack Brown watched until he was out of sight.

Back in the hut, Barlow was stretching out the wings of the bird as if he was trying to teach it to fly.

Do you think it's a sign, Jack Brown?

Yep, said Jack Brown. *One day we're all gonna go the way of the bird.*

We're going to fly?

Jack Brown could not hold himself back any longer. He picked up Barlow by the neck of his shirt and pressed him against the wall and said, *If you don't get yourself together, you are going to die.*

Barlow's face was a parade of expressions. First, a gasping, indignant shock and then cheeks colored with anger, warping into an odd, juvenile expression that Jack Brown did not know how to respond to. But then Barlow broke into a sobbing, *I don't want to die. I just want to find her.*

Jack Brown dropped Barlow and he crumpled on the ground.

Give up that shit you're on.

I can't do it on my own. I need your help.

It's not my job.

It's your job to help me.

I'm the tracker, not your nurse.

Just give me a week. Throw me in the cell. Give me food and water and for fuck's sake don't open the door.

The third night in the cell, Barlow screamed out to Jack Brown, *Get her out! She's under my bed. Her bony fucking finger is tracing down my back.*

Jack Brown was dressed in his underpants but he went into the cell anyway. He lit a candle and waved it under Barlow's bed. There was nothing there. He swiped his hand beneath it to show Barlow but when he looked up Barlow was gone.

The back door of the hut was wide open and Jack Brown could see Barlow running through the grass, crying, *She's gonna fucking get me!*

Jack Brown chased him down the slope and tackled him to the ground.

She's there, I know she's fucking in there. She's got this screwed-up face and I can feel her finger in my back and she was pulling at my hair and—

Jack Brown punched Barlow and knocked him out. He carried him back inside and laid him down on the bed in the cell.

That night he sat on the veranda, listening to Barlow's moaning.

What good is a sergeant? he thought. *And what good is a sergeant who has lost his mind?*

Two days later Barlow was quiet in his cell. Jack Brown gave him food through the bars and Barlow said, *I think it's over.*

We'll head off at first light tomorrow, then, said Jack Brown.

Jack Brown wasted no time. He got on his horse and rode to Lay Ping. He undressed her and ran his hands over her back and traced the figures tattooed across her shoulders and down her spine.

There was a god and goddess, deities that he did not know or recognize. They were bearing down on a waterfall and within the waterfall was everything they had given life to: all mountains, all rocks, all creatures, all sliding down into the dip of her back and her hips.

And then: SORROW.

Who is this? he said, touching the god on her shoulder, whose eyes were inflamed with rage.

This is I{ʒ}anagi, said Lay Ping as she twisted her long hair around her hand. *He is in a fit of jealousy and soon he will tumble into the waterfall and sink down into the world beneath the rocks.*

And what happens there? asked Jack Brown.

He will be eaten by demons.

Jack Brown lay on the bed. And then Lay Ping lay on top of him. He closed his eyes. There he saw the world beneath the rocks, the world that her skin did not reveal.

*T*he station owner of Phantom Ridge did not wait for Barlow, the big-city sergeant, to take any action at all. He had his men post Wanted signs of Jessie around the valley. They collected a wedding photo from the postmaster. There never looked a bride more unhappy. Her dark eyes were narrowed and her disheveled hair only partly hid the bruises taking shape on her forehead and cheek.

They nailed posters to trees, and others they strung to fences with wire. Even before the men rode away, the posters turned crisp with the unseasonable heat and seemed to fade before their eyes, but they did not fade so much that the reward was no longer visible. Anyone could make out that the capture of this woman with dark eyes and long dark hair was worth one thousand pounds to someone. There was no fine print regarding who had offered the reward or who would ever pay it, but many of those who saw it had a mind for pictures and numbers only. The money itself was enough to impress itself upon them, and in a day or two the news had spread to the single cabins, where all the men, who were otherwise tapping mugs on their tables or skinning some bony thing for their dinner, took the news as they would take a gold nugget between their teeth and they felt it like a tweaked nerve changing their fortunes forever.

In their minds there was no shadow of a doubt that Jessie was the thief and a murderer, too. Some of them knew Fitz firsthand to be a drunk and, worse, a boastful drunk, bragging about the ways he might kill her. But who were they to judge? If they held to an eye for an eye as their order of justice, most of them would be blind anyway. The thought of weighing up a man's sins against the way he should die unnerved them and their sympathy swung to Fitz and was ignited more by the thought of him dying by the hand of a woman. And, further, they considered the size of Fitz and the force of him and what they knew of her and they concluded her powers must be unnatural. His house was burnt down and his body was not found and they preferred to think of witchcraft rather than the idea that there was some accomplice among them. Those who had a head for it deduced that Fitz's stockman Jack Brown and the rabble-rousers Fitz recruited job to job had been sent up north to deliver cattle, so that left only her and her carefully chosen moment.

There was talk that cattle were disappearing without a trace and the old man, too, gave fuel to the story. He reported that since Jessie had passed through his house in her escape to the mountains, the old woman, his wife, was no longer sane and had begun muttering prayers when she thought that he could not hear her. She had never prayed aloud, not in all the years he had known her, only to herself. And so, in no time at all, the posters and the talk together inspired a terrible scourge and they believed that they were armed with enough reasons for capturing and killing my mother.

Most of them rode in packs, partly because they did not know the terrain of the mountains, but more out of superstition. Some of them had lived in the shadow of the mountains for more years than they had fingers, but still the mountains sat unnamed and until now the men had no reason to go near them. Only for the fact of the reward money did some ride entirely alone. But they were few, having no assurance that if they fell or lost their footing they would ever be found.

THE OLD WOMAN HEARD THEM in the night, a cacophony of horses and men. Metal and leather slapping against horses' bellies, tins and pots and guns, men reckless and howling.

She rose from the bed she shared with the old man and took pains to be quiet, though now it seemed that nothing would wake him. She shuffled out, collecting her shawl and her boots, and moved into the dark to where his dog was tied to a tree. The dog's eyes glistened, moving like two flames in his head, and as she came up beside him she cooed so he would not bark but then he did. She used the words the old man used, *Shush, you mongrel bastard*, and then she muzzled the dog as she had seen the old man do, wrapping rope around his snout. The muzzling sent him bracing against the tree in a soundless fit, his eyes protruding for all he could not bark.

The old woman walked towards the fence until she could see the men riding in the distance. Some of them carried lanterns, and from afar and part illuminated they appeared wrongly composed, the neck of a horse joined with the face of a man, long arms holding lanterns. The old woman could not determine how many they numbered but from the racket she thought them to be a small army.

She stood deathly still in the paddock and watched them pass and as they moved it was like watching a creature hurrying in the night towards its kill. When she could no longer see them, she could hear them groaning and then the slowing of their horses when they reached the slope of the mountain.

She knew the price that was on Jessie's head and she knew that it made no difference to men like that if they killed her. There was life in Jessie. Even when my mother was on the cusp of death the old woman had seen it in her. The old woman did not know what she would make of that life but she knew that it was worth more than the price they had put on my mother.

She opened the gate of the paddock that faced the mountains and returned to the dog, who was still fitting by the tree. She untied the rope at the tree and with a flick of her wrist unwound the muzzle. Unleashed, the dog sprinted out into the dark. The men had left their keen scent in the air and turned-up earth with the bolting of their horses. The old woman knew that the dog would track them and finally meet them farther up the mountains. She hoped that the yellow-eyed dog would be read as a terrifying omen and she prayed that there were at least some among them who would take heed of such a warning.

*I*t was evening when the gang arrived back at the camp and the boy was waiting for them on the ridge. Above him it looked as though the clouds had captured the sun and everything was pink and luminous.

The gang was exhausted by the ride, Jessie included, and as soon as they had secured the wild horses in the holding yard and fed and watered their own, they flopped down by the fire the boy had started and gazed up at the sky. The clouds were moving fast and no cloud was still for long enough that any of them could make it out as any earthly or mythical creature.

Jessie rested her head against her arm and watched the boy preparing their meal by the fire. His beauty, the gang, the clouds, all of it seemed miraculous, all of it incomprehensible.

THE NEXT DAY the rope they had carried back to the camp was strung up to a tree and a pulley; they attached a branch for a handle and a seat and a flying fox was made. The boy went first, launching himself from the ridge, and he flew from one side of the camp to the other. They spent the whole day running back and forth and none of them seemed to be tired from it or even tired from the day before. Jessie watched them from the shade and she loved the boy's expression most of all as he sailed through the air, his eyes as wide as his smile, growing less fearful with each ride.

VI

IV

J ack Brown and Barlow set off at first light, the way any expedition should, their packs loaded with supplies, their hats on their heads, rifles slung across their backs. Jack Brown felt fit and ready for it, released from some great tension that had been holding him back from lighting out these last months and finding Jessie himself. Barlow seemed edgy in his saddle, but the day unfolded in silence and neither man knew what the other was thinking.

It wasn't until halfway into the day that Barlow said, *I need to eat,* and Jack Brown urged him to keep riding till they reached the river. Barlow didn't argue or say anything but fell in behind Jack Brown's horse and followed him closely, in what Jack Brown took to be a sulk.

If I have to stop suddenly your horse's nose will be up my arse.

Barlow slipped farther back for a while but then Jack Brown could feel him stepping up close again, and when he couldn't stand it any longer Jack Brown pulled his horse right up and Barlow had to swing his horse out, tearing at its neck suddenly and pulling it wide. Jack Brown rode on. Barlow tried to settle his horse and soon Jack Brown spotted a tree with enough shade for them both to sit down in with some distance from each other.

Riding towards it, Jack Brown could see a poster nailed to the trunk. He dismounted and tore the poster down.

Jessie, he said, and the breath went out of him as his gut turned over. *Fuck*, he said to himself, and then he yelled to Barlow, *They've put a fucking bounty on her head.*

Barlow rode up next to Jack Brown and Jack Brown handed him the poster.

It's not legal, said Barlow.

It doesn't fucking matter. They've named the prize. It's like unleashing dogs on her.

Let's keep steady, said Barlow. *We've got to eat, and the horses need to rest.* He dismounted.

This is fucked, said Jack Brown. *They'll already be out for her. If I wasn't wiping your arse, I would have been out here much sooner.*

Bullshit, said Barlow, tightening the straps on his saddle. *There was nothing stopping you going after her from the day she disappeared.*

Jack Brown unbuckled his saddlebag and slumped to the ground while his horse took to grazing around him. He unwrapped the loaf of bread he had bought from the cook at the Seven Sisters. It was as heavy as a brick. He tore off a hunk of it and pushed it into his mouth, which was wet with saliva not from hunger but from a sudden feeling of sickness. He chewed with his mouth open and as he chewed he surveyed the field they had ridden across. The long grass was bleached white by the sun and it collapsed as the wind traveled over it and sprang back as the wind turned in front of them.

For the rest of the day Jack Brown set an urgent pace unless they were riding through thick forest. They did not see a living thing, aside from birds that swooped in and stripped the trees as they rode. Jack Brown felt them to be riding in the wake of a storm that had recently passed through and he shuddered to think of the groups of men taking to the mountain like hungry dogs and the murderous intent they carried inside them.

That night they slid off their horses and walked, chafed and bowlegged, to set up camp next to the river. Jack Brown limped to the water and dunked his head right in and saw there were bream, silver and fat and feeding at the edges. He fashioned a net by tying his shirt to a stick and caught two of them.

He threw the fish at Barlow. *Here. I'm not gonna be your hunter-gatherer and your cook, too.*

He settled himself by the fire that Barlow had lit and watched as Barlow began to clean the fish. Silver scales sprayed up against his hands and stuck to the shirtsleeves that he hadn't bothered to roll up.

Been to see the Sisters lately? said Barlow.

You just ate their bread.

Did you pay for it?

Actually, you did.

Did you stay?

What business is that of yours, Sergeant?

I just want to know if we should bill the Crown for your fuck.

What can I say, Sergeant? God save the King.

Did the King suck your cock?

Jack Brown lay down, the bridge of his back against the curve of his saddle. He tipped his hat low till he could see only the flickering light of the fire and Barlow's bare feet stepping around it. He could not ward off the feeling that he should have left sooner, and already he wanted to ditch his companion.

He was woken by Barlow kicking the sole of his boot and handing him a plate of fish and the remainder of the bread, which he had toasted in the fire. The fire was blazing and stacked up like a pyramid. It smoked thick and black and Jack Brown was about to tell Barlow to kick it down and use fewer leaves, for the way it smoked and spat and surely signaled their coming. But then he thought better of it. It was better that he forewarn her, signal their slow ascent.

He believed they would not find her if she did not want to be found.

That night he dreamt of her stalking through the caves in the mountains above him—which part of the mountains he could not tell—and he looked for where the sun might be and for some signs, as if even in his dreams he knew to look. Then he saw what surrounded the caves—an impassable ravine filled with the crumpled bodies of horses and men. All of their legs snapped and pointing at angles, like broken trees littered on the ground.

THE GANGS OF MEN crashed up the mountainside, splitting into groups of four and five, scything through the bush in different directions, paying no heed to existing tracks or openings but all seemingly possessed to forge a course of their own devising. The dog charged up the mountain after them, more nimble than a horse. When he finally caught up with one of the packs, he got under the feet of a horse, which bucked and threw its rider. The man tumbled screaming into a canyon and his screaming and the dog's barking caused other horses to buck until only one man of the party remained in the saddle. That man raised his gun to shoot the dog, which sent him running through the bush in pursuit of another party.

*T*he mountain range was an amphitheater and the sounds below were delivered up the mountainside through slow and echoing time, but in time enough.

The boy eased himself down from his watch and ran silently through the bush. Barefoot, he padded over turns in the earth and rocks that glittered with mica. He knew the others would be sleeping.

The sounds he had heard were unmistakable. The crashing of the forest, the sound of men on a hunt. These were men made confident of their catch only by their numbers and not by the design of their pursuit and they signaled themselves as clearly as spot fires moving up the mountain.

Running, the boy felt spiderwebs crisscrossing between the lower shrubs and branches and collecting around the bare skin of his arms and face. He did not pause but kept on running, brushing the webs as he ran.

The gang all knew of his nightly surveillance. As he did not ride and did not muster, it was his contribution to the camp. The main danger, he thought, was at night, while they slept. It was surely when the worst things from the valley could move up the mountain undetected.

The sun was just up when he reached the camp and Joe was saddling a horse with Bill.

They're coming. The boy was breathless.

Who?

There's heaps of them.

Where?

Up from the valley.

Get on.

Joe mounted his horse and pulled the boy up behind him. Bill did not waste time in saddling but followed on her own horse.

They rode to the lookout and, though they could not see them, Joe and Bill heard for themselves the unnatural cracking of branches below as the large party moved up from the mountain.

That's the sound of a desperate man, said Joe.

I know this type of man, said Bill. *He has no god. And he is all the more dangerous to us because, worse than that, he has no law in him or myth to live by.*

When Jessie woke, they were all sitting around on the dirt with their heads hanging between their bony knees, wearing the crumpled clothes they had worn the day before and then slept in. Joe was squatting, drawing a map on the ground that looked like two hands crossing over, the fingers interlocking. His face was knotted and serious.

He was saying, *From what we know of the caves and tunnels, we can enter here and come out here, which will bring us to the other side. But while it is narrow and well concealed I cannot say if the horses will travel the whole way through.*

What's this? said Jessie.

There's a gang moving up the mountain, seems they've split into packs. The boy spotted them on his watch this morning. We can't risk them finding us here.

I heard 'em traveling up, miss, said the boy. *They were making a racket, splitting branches with what sounds like blades and guns and mallets.*

Jessie felt sick to her stomach. The thought of violent men discovering the boy, or any of them, was more horror than she could bear to imagine. Whether they were in pursuit of her for Fitz's murder or all of them for the stolen cattle at Phantom Ridge, it did not matter. She would do anything to stop them.

Sit down with us, Jessie, said Joe. *Help us plan our escape.*

There's tunnels out and down and there's a way we can all get clear of them, said Bill. *We've got enough lead and there's chambers beneath us and we can clear out and take the route that Joe knows. We can hide in there for days and listen to them pass over us or we can press on, we can keep going to the other side of the mountains.*

You can all do that, said Jessie as she sat down next to the boy and, taking a small stick, began to draw her own map on the dirt. *But it is me they are after. I have done something unspeakable in the valley and I will not risk any of you for the sake of my own freedom. I'll meet them halfway down the mountain, and if I can I'll draw them in a chase back towards the valley. If you hide or travel further on for a while, you will be able to return here eventually.*

But we are a gang, miss. We do not sacrifice one for another, said Joe.

I am sure it is me they want, said Jessie. *I will not have any of you running on behalf of me.*

They all got busy disassembling the camp, starting at its perimeter and moving in. Its perimeter was marked on one side by the places they inhabited—the camp, the garden, the holding yard—and on the other side by a plummeting cliff. They moved in, not hand in hand but linked well enough by their purpose. First they destroyed the holding yard by breaking down the woven branches with their feet and throwing them in every direction.

They moved to the garden then, setting aside what produce they could, then turning over the soil so the garden would reveal nothing of itself. Despite their labor the soil was still a mesh of roots and green leaves and rich with dung. If one of the riders came upon the camp and ran his fingers through the soil, its richness and darkness would hint at their presence. But now there was no time to conceal it otherwise, no time to bury the dirt itself, so they moved in towards the center of the camp, pulling down hessian curtains and collecting in their arms anything that further told of them, separating it into two piles, one to pack and one to hide. All of it would have burnt easily as a pyre, but they could not risk it flaming up, signaling their position at the top of the mountain. So what they could not pack they rolled up and buried in the dark recesses of a cave, where they knew that no impatient man would bother to look.

When the camp was finally turned over and hidden, they stood again at the place where they had gathered earlier in the morning, around what was left of Joe's drawing on the ground. They squatted over it, as if trying to catch a closer look at their unknown future, and it was the boy who was the first to cry. Bill put her arm around him.

There's not time to waste with crying now, said Joe. *It's a long way down and we can shed our tears as we go. Grab your saddles, gang, and divide this load among you. Bill, can you double the boy?*

Jessie made a pack for herself and then she saddled up Houdini. She rested against him for a while and watched the gang. She knew it could be the last time she would ever see them. She savored glimpses of them, their young hands passing things between them as if each thing were a gift in itself—a bridle, a rope, a tin. Each gesture between them looked to her to be a thing of grace.

When the gang was close to heading down, she led Houdini to the boy and said, *This is my only possession on earth and now I want you to own him. I know you are not fond of riding but, I promise you, Houdini will never let you down, as long as you care for him.*

The boy did not say a word but took the reins from her hand and with her help mounted Houdini. He looked so light and small on Houdini's back.

Miss, he said, *I believe you. Now will you walk us out? Me and Houdini and Ned?*

Jessie walked close to Houdini, and the boy's dog trailed them. She walked slowly down the track to the ridge where Joe and the others were gathering.

Soon all their horses were lined up on the edge of the ridge. Jessie looked out beyond them. Here was a sky rippling without end. She patted Houdini and squeezed the boy's ankle and said, *Love him*, and the boy said, *I will.*

She made her way along the line to Joe, who was leaning down from his horse and offering his hand. She took it in both of hers.

You are a good man, Joe, she said. *Thank you for counting me as one of you.*

You are one of us, said Joe, and he took back his hand and swung his horse out and stepped it down the ridge with the others to follow.

Bill went next and she winked at Jessie and smiled. *Maybe next time you see me, I'll have grown my hair and I'll not call myself Bill.*

Bill is as fine a name as anyone could want, given or chosen, said Jessie. *You can call yourself whatever you want now. Whatever feels true.*

Miss Jessie, said Bill. She halted on the ridge. *Remember that man chasing you? He cannot reach you.* Bill pointed upwards. *Look at Pleiades. That man, he's already locked in the sky.*

I will miss you, said Jessie.

Bill nodded and moved her horse down and the others followed close behind. Jessie stepped back to let them pass. She sat and watched as each horse and rider disappeared below the ridgeline. When they were all out of sight, she listened to the scraping of hooves on the rocks and the sound of hooves folding in among other hooves.

She took a branch from the ground and, stepping back the way she had come, swept away their tracks all the way back to the camp, where there was nothing left but her knife, her gun and the small pack she had saved. She walked to the lookout and stationed herself there, listening for the sounds of men moving up the other side of the mountain. She looked down on the rocks and the trees and all the things under the sun that would outlast her or any of them. Within the trees now, she knew, was everything that she had ever wished to escape from, all violence and all fear. It had multiplied and was moving up the mountain to find her.

She listened for them. She listened with all of her intent but there was a sound that echoed in her head. It was the words she had just spoken—*I will miss you.*

SHE MOVED DOWN.

She did not make fires in the day but allowed herself only a small fire at night to cook a snake or wallaby or any edible creature that she caught. She did not use her gun but hunted in silence with her knife or her hands. When she came upon a snake she would grab its tail from behind and snap its neck, as clean as she would crack a whip, and that was the most noise she made. She was cautious of killing legged creatures for their screeching as they fought, but if they were in sight and, better, within reach, she killed them as swiftly and as quietly as she could.

She slept in caves or upon some scrubby surface, any place that would not hold her impression or give her away. She walked, when she could, in darkness and she found a pace that was almost silent. Most days she walked barefoot carrying her boots under her arms in case she came across anything she could eat and needed to save. She walked for so long that there were moments she forgot why she was walking at all. But then the birds would sound loudly at some point in the day, as if their calls were a warning and she must remember to listen beyond them for the sounds of men riding solo and in packs.

She walked on stealthily, disturbing nothing that she did not want to eat. She felt herself to be no more than a two-legged creature, roaming and hunting and sleeping. She moved along, one foot, then the other. She thought that even animals must sense their fate, and as she had seen, some of them did not run from it. If death was to be her fate, she would not deny it, nor would she put her head straight into its mouth. She imagined herself then to be one of those creatures whose nature was not to run from death, but to run alongside it.

J ack Brown and Barlow rode into the mountains and the mountains rose up around them. Jack Brown could see a confusion of tracks and he wondered how long it would take for the tracks to sink into the earth or be blown clean. He was aware, as they rode, that they were leaving their own tracks, too. And as they rode higher and higher into the mountains they were being remembered by some lost world, some world beyond time.

It was nothing he could name or describe to Barlow.

You don't have to find someone dead in their tracks to prove it was their tracks, was all he said, from sunup to sundown. He swayed them towards the highest mountain. Barlow trailed behind.

*T*he night was too bright to walk unobserved so Jessie slept in a cave. She wound her hair up and used it to pillow her head against the rock. She slept easily and dreamt of a swirling universe, and when she woke she did not know what it was or why she saw it. She lay in the cave that was still dark, well concealed as it was from the sun that had already risen, that its shallow entrance did not allow in. Her blood surged as she heard voices. Frozen in fear, one ear to the rock, the other to the hollow and dark of the cave. The voices folded around her. They were loud but she could not tell what they were saying. She waited, pressing against the rock, not daring to breathe until the voices passed, waiting until she could hear nothing but the birds cawing into the day.

IT WAS BROAD DAYLIGHT as she tracked them but she could have tracked them in the deepest dark with a mile between them. There were four of them and they rode messy and loud and she could not imagine how they would have found her unless they had tripped over her, which they almost did. She followed them all day as they warred against the bush with their blades and their guns, as if the trees themselves were another and certain enemy. By early afternoon she could tell they were worn-out. From behind she could see them, woozy and swaying, their weapons slack against their calves.

She walked at a pace that relied on them moving steadily. Some of the ground was uneven and patchy with branches they had cut down, and these sliced her feet and sounded her steps and she felt the tension of having to keep a distance so they would not hear her.

When it was dark she moved closer in and hid in the low scrub. They lit a fire and the smell of something cooking on it turned her stomach for her hunger. She chewed on a bit of bark, then spat it out so it did not splinter in her throat.

She could hear them shouting at one another. She could see them, through the split of branches, their faces lit up, the four of them. She watched them, and when their shouting dropped away, she feared they had spotted her.

She waited but nothing happened. She looked again. She hoped they had passed out. She could see only one of them who was still upright, his arms folded across his chest. She was not close enough to tell if he was sleeping or watching the fire.

She waited until she could not wait anymore. Her feet were itchy with scratches and she was too hungry to be still. She crawled in closer, close enough to see the horses were tied up in a cluster but on the other side of the men.

She began to step around the outside of their camp in a wide arc, but without the cover of their movements and their shouting the bush made so much noise that she was sure to wake them. She could go out wider but now, closer in, she could see that they were camped beneath a ledge of rock and she determined that she could shuffle over it and climb down behind their horses. She strapped her gun down her back and tied her knife to her arm but her boots would drag on the rock so she left them behind.

She crawled to the ledge, sacrificing skin for silence as her knees and elbows took the brunt of her slow, dragging movements. From the ledge, she could see all of them. She could not see the faces of the ones lying down, but the one sitting up looked ghastly; his head was back and his mouth was open and he need only open one eye to be looking directly at her.

She tried to stay back in the shadows, but even the shadows were well lit by the bright sky and the ledge was close enough that she could feel the heat of their campfire. She crawled on. When she was above their horses she began to claw down the face of the rock, hoping with each step down that her hands and feet would find another groove close enough so she did not have to jump.

When her feet touched the ground, the earth was warmer and more comforting than anything she had felt. She surveyed their horses and began to soothe the best-looking one, patting its neck, lowering her eyes. She swung herself up. And then, taking its mane, she set off, right through the camp, the fastest way out of there, heading towards the track she had followed them on all day.

She did not look back but knew the sound of the horse splitting through their camp would wake them. She bolted down the uneven track as fast as she could and for a moment was grateful for the almost-full moon that lit the track. But then she heard a shot and she knew that in this light her back would be as visible as the moon itself and though she only heard one shot, she knew it would not be the last. Death was on her.

J ack Brown and Barlow thought they heard the lowing of cattle as they traveled up the mountain, but moving farther up, towards the source of the sound, they realized it was not cattle they heard. The sound seemed to come from inside the mountain itself. It was shifting and strange. Eventually they explained it away as the wind blowing through splices of rock and that same wind pushing and echoing into deeper chambers.

They rode on.

They saw no human or horse tracks. It was late in the day when Jack Brown spotted a path to a stony ridge that led up to the mouth of a cave. They secured their horses with rope to a tree and then began to climb up the ridge that was steep and loose with rocks. Their boots were made for riding horses, not climbing ridges, so they slipped and scrambled, taking turns to offer a hand up or find a foothold. By the time they reached the lip of the ridge they were sweating and panting and their fingers smarted from clinging to the rock face. They heaved themselves up over the top of the ridge and as they sighted the opening of the cave, a huge bird flew out of it and swiped their heads.

Fuck me! What was that? said Barlow.

I don't fucking know, said Jack Brown. *But it fucking parted the hair on my head and the hair on my arse as well.*

They sat panting on the ridge like two old men, watching the bird fly out over the escarpment. Despite its size, it soon disappeared from view.

They were cautious about entering the cave. Barlow lit a match and held it out in front of him, which did little to illuminate the darkness of the cave.

Get a couple going so we can take a look inside, said Jack Brown.

Barlow lit more matches and carried them like a torch in front of him. They moved in slowly.

They could not tell what they were stepping over but the ground crunched underfoot. The matches soon burnt down, and in attempting to light more, Barlow dropped the packet on the ground. The total darkness played tricks on their eyes and Jack Brown thought he saw the form of a sleeping child and then, farther on, the movement of bodies against the cave wall.

Will you light the bloody things? said Jack Brown.

Barlow was patting around, searching for the packet of matches. He finally found it and lit two more.

Someone has been here, said Jack Brown. He felt the floor of the cave and it felt warm to him, as if someone had just been sleeping there.

I'm getting the fuck out, said Barlow. *I'm going to camp outside.*

I'm gonna sleep in here, said Jack Brown.

That night Jack Brown was happy to be inside the cave without the fitful moanings and exclamations of Barlow waking him. He dragged his swag in as far as he could while still able to see the opening of the cave. He lay back and listened. The mountain sounded discordant and strange. With his head upon it, the lowing was amplified. Being inside it he could imagine it better, the wind passing through its tunnels and chambers. He gave his mind to it and he imagined that the source of the sound was not the wind but the wind was merely the carrier and what he actually heard was the echo of past inhabitants. And maybe they had not passed at all but the sound he heard was human voices freshly created.

In his time in the valley he had heard drovers talking. Some of them said that the tribes in the mountains had moved on, but there were a few who said that the tribes remained and that they defended the mountains. There was one drover whose voice he could still hear: *As black as those men are, they can make themselves invisible and you will only see them as they lean over you to kill you.*

Jack Brown did not know what of it might be true. He suspected the drovers made things up for their own entertainment. He'd listened to the talk of men around a fire that sounded to him as fanciful as something from a children's storybook. What he knew for sure was that he himself was descended in part from one of the tribes that they spoke of. If he had inherited from either his droving father or his domestic mother an inclination to kill, for all the times he had imagined killing Fitz he did not do it. They were the times he wished he was more possessed of killing than was actually in him, wherever it came from.

He wondered who had camped here last. If it was Jessie. And who had lain here before her. Had they contemplated the sounds that echoed inside the mountains? What stories had they made of them?

Jack Brown was overwhelmed by the thought of it. And soon the thoughts turned to feeling and he could not bear to think of anything else on earth disappearing. Whether it be tribe or man or woman, he could not bear to think of anything of fight or spirit vanishing into rock. He hoped that within the mountain there was indeed a tribe and they were safe in secret places, and if this was their cave, he hoped, too, that they would forgive his trespass upon it.

*T*he boy had shown her a gorge and she led the hunters to it. The only way to lose them was through tougher and tougher terrain, and yet she could not lead them back up the mountain for fear they would discover the campsite or any sign of the gang. And she knew she could not lead them directly down into the valley to be fired at without cover or protection in the open fields.

The gorge was narrow and dark and promised a steep decline and an uneven surface, then the surprise of rushing water. She ripped along the track, weighing its danger. Three hunters on her trail, if they hadn't collected more. Three armed riders with nothing to lose except the horses they rode. It would be worth it, even to lose one of them.

She pushed on in the dark, finding her way around trees that shone back silver. She could smell the water of the gorge carried up the warm cliffs and she breathed it in. The track vanished and she plummeted down into the deep canyon. She laid herself flat on the stolen horse and tried not to give herself away by screaming out the fear that was in her.

The horse flew down the slope and did not stop. It could not have, even if it wanted to. The drop passed as a terror and she did not know if beneath them was rock or dirt or air or what the horse was even holding on to. The horse skidded down and she breathed relief when the horse's neck evened out and it found its feet. She pulled herself up to sitting.

She heard them then. All three hunters flinging themselves down the same drop. She pushed the horse into the water and rode through, not stopping for the horse to balance but holding its neck pointed to the other side so it had no choice but to get there. She heard the men hitting the water and the screaming of a man as he lost his horse and panicked. From the continued surging sound of the water she knew his companions had not stopped to save him.

She crossed the water and pelted on through the thick scrub, pushing her body right down against the neck of the horse. Its heart was pounding. She urged it on and, though it did not stop and she did not turn back, in her mind she could see the man left behind in the river. The man was grabbing for a stick and, finding the stick without buoyancy, wrestled with it until his shirt and coat twisted up and drowned him.

That night, Barlow was sick of the sight of Jack Brown's head. He lodged himself outside the cave and by the light of the sky he tried to write in his empty journal. But as he pressed down, the nib of his pen snapped, and where he wanted words on the page there was only a blob of ink. He had thought that this would be his story to tell, a young sergeant capturing an infamous female bushranger. But he had no spare nib to write the story and there was still no certain sign of her.

In truth, he felt far from victory or hope. Days and days of sitting on his horse directed by whatever sign that Jack Brown intuited had bred an impatience and, later, a hostile anger in him, a force of rage he had not ever felt or expected to feel.

He closed his journal and lay down on his swag to sleep but was kept awake by the involuntary grinding of his teeth. He twisted and arched his back and neck and kicked his legs under a blanket, trying to get the feeling out of him.

All day he had watched Jack Brown, easy and relaxed in his saddle, sun slick, his hands floating on his knees, his body moving as if it were another muscular extension of the body of the horse. Looking this way, looking that, coming out with grand statements beyond rhyme or reason, like he always knew something that Barlow did not.

For Barlow, the mountains had unfolded without meaning. The colors and shapes continued to be strange to him and as they had moved higher up the slope he felt the clouds weighing in like the ceiling of a room that was sinking down upon him.

All day he saw silver leaves as bullets shooting through the trees and though he wore his badge visible and shiny with its eagle sweeping in, it seemed ridiculous when they saw no one, and he knew the badge itself would not deflect a bullet once a gun was aimed at him.

He lay there, his heart racing from the spasms of his body, the kicking and the snapping of his legs. He knew there was every chance he might die before he saw her again, that bullet or cliff could claim him and he would never get to see her as a grown woman, or reproach and punish her for deserting him. He knew that he might die with her only as a recurring dream and a recurring nightmare of Miss Jessie leaving Bandy Arrow.

Jessie was cold and wet and frantic. She had survived the gorge but her mind was blank and she had no knowledge of the terrain on the other side of it. There were still two men on her trail and she knew that by pushing forward she was only marking a path for them to follow. She could hear the wheezing of their frightened horses and yet they pushed on as she did, reckless as hell in the dark. It was almost too close to continue.

She rode on anyway, searching below her. All she could see was the shiny surface of the rock face disappearing into darkness. She guessed it was slippery with moss and water. But she had to climb down it. She pulled up the horse suddenly and swung to the ground. With a slap she sent it back in the hunters' direction. At best they would think she had been bucked, falling to her death. At worst they would think she had been unseated and would still come after her. She knew they would not risk leaving their horses and there was no way of traveling down the rock face on horseback unless they were intent on their own suicide. Better if they were.

She rolled up her trousers and emptied the bullets out of her gun in case she slipped and fired it. She strapped it again to her back and she began to scale down. Her hands and feet clung to clumps of moss and twisted vines and roots that grew out of the rock.

Silently she went. She could not hear the hunters, so she carried on, moving down, clutching at whatever she could, whatever nature offered her. She stopped when she heard them above her, pressed her face and body against the rock and waited for them to pass. She could not risk a loose rock giving her away.

As she held on, her legs began to tremble with exhaustion. She clenched them to stop them shaking and then a feeling like pins and needles set into her feet and they finally grew numb.

The hunters passed. She kicked her feet against the rock to prompt her blood's return to them. She trusted only the grip of her hands although they were damp with sweat. She wiped them on her shirt and began to lower herself down again, her hands taking most of her weight.

It worked, this lowering down, the weight of her in her hands, and she could even see an end in sight as the cliff gave way to ground. But the rope of the vine she clung to snapped. Her feet had no hold and twisted out and slipped, her gun, her shirt, all sliding up around her, her bare skin scraping against the rock. She tried to grab for moss or rock or vine, anything, but nature seemed to balk. There was nothing to hold on to.

She fell and fell until the cliff finally turned her out on a ledge. She landed feetfirst and then crumpled down with the shock of it. She was conscious, she was on the ground, her body was shaking. And then, the most surprising thing, her body in its shock began to shudder with laughter.

Fuck me, she said.

She sat down, tried to straighten her legs, to stretch out. She felt her back. It was warm and damp and when she tasted her fingers, she tasted blood. She had no cloth to bind herself but her shirt, which she could not sacrifice by ripping it up. She knew when blood and skin meshed with fabric it could be worse than the wound itself, so she took off her shirt and let the night air cool and dry the cuts.

She waited. Still and silent on the ground. She consoled herself that maybe in the fall she had gained a couple of hours, even half a day or night, from her hunters.

When the blood on her back was dry enough, she put back on her scrap of a shirt and realized the ground she was on was actually another, shorter ledge. She climbed down from it, though it would have been shallow enough to jump, and found herself on a track. She walked along, her whole body stiff and sore, carrying her rifle, charged somehow by the adrenaline of her fall and her survival.

She walked through the night.

When she made out the two distinct forms standing on the track she thought she must have been hallucinating. But as she moved closer, it was clear. There were two saddled horses tied up to a tree. One of them she recognized, absolutely.

And then terror struck—the old man's dog was moving towards her and growling—and above her someone yelled, *Miss Jessie*.

She looked up and saw a ghost and the ghost was holding a gun and the ghost was all grown up.

And then all stars and dust and hope and loss came crashing together at once as the dog leapt on Jessie, and Bandy Arrow fired.

*B*arlow had the dog in his sights first. He was already awake and alert to every strange sound. He heard the dog moving through the bush. The dog was growling. He did not know what wild dogs roamed the mountains, if they came in packs, what they might do to him or the horses. He did not waste time wondering. He loaded his gun and crawled to the ridgeline.

He did not expect to see her. But there she was, standing near the horses, bailed up by the dog. Finally he had her.

His hand was trembling as he trained his gun on the dog and then on Jessie. Both were oblivious to him. He stood and yelled out, *Miss Jessie*. The dog barked and the horses reared. She grabbed her gun from her back as the dog leapt on her and locked his jaw around some part of her.

Barlow aimed at the dog. He took a shot. The dog unhooked itself from Jessie's arm and went for the horses. He took another shot. Jessie fell down and so did Jack Brown's horse.

Jack Brown appeared on the ledge in time to see Jessie and his horse collapsing.

What the fuck have you done? he said.

Jessie was loading her gun on the ground. Her arm was bleeding profusely. She pointed the gun at the top of the ridge.

Put the gun down, said Barlow.

Jessie!

Jack Brown?

Do as Barlow says.

Why should I?

He's the law, Jessie.

Jessie put the gun down and watched the two men climb down the rock.

There was nothing more to fear. Both her ghosts had caught her, both her ghosts were strapping her arm, both her ghosts were helping her to her feet.

T hey set off down the mountain, Barlow doubling Jessie on his own horse and Jack Brown trailing behind them. Barlow had offered his horse to Jack Brown and Jack Brown had refused it. Jessie suggested that the two men should double each other and she could walk. But neither of them would have it, especially Barlow, who foresaw her escaping.

Barlow said, *You know that if you do try to escape, you will only be hunted by packs of men and they do not care if they bring you back to the valley dead or alive. For what it is worth, we are your best chance of surviving.*

What about Jack Brown? said Jessie.

I will walk down, said Jack Brown. *If there is a shortcut, I'll take it and I will meet you at the bottom of the casing.*

The track narrowed as it wound down and Barlow and Jessie disappeared ahead of Jack Brown.

He was sulking, which he was not proud of, and he let the space between them lengthen. He had supposed Barlow's shooting of his horse was deliberate and, thinking about it more, he concluded that it was—that now Barlow had found Jessie, there was no use for him. He felt shafted by both of them, that Barlow's offering of his horse was just a hollow attempt to save face. Jessie gave little away and he had no way of knowing what she was thinking or how she was planning to escape this time or if she was planning an escape at all. He could tell there was some history between her and Barlow, some recognition. He felt jealous of it and he hated that they were now riding together in front of him. It all swilled inside him and became an ache in his gut and he thought of deserting them both and disappearing into the mountains. He did not know why he was following them. What good could come of it now?

But the thought of Jessie out there in front of him, possibly in danger, kept him walking. He picked up a branch and threw it out against the drop of the cliff in a futile but satisfying gesture.

He walked on.

Jessie and Barlow rode along the slowly descending track with Jessie turning her head at each bend to see if Jack Brown was following.

He won't lose us, said Barlow. *He's the tracker.*

It made Jessie anxious not to see Jack Brown, not to know if he was actually following them directly. What was his intention? And what was Bandy Arrow's? Her head was spinning.

I know who you are, she said.

You recognized me?

You look the same.

I'm not Bandy Arrow and I'm not seven years old.

What happened to you? You're a fucking cop?

I was adopted by a police sergeant and his wife, who were there the night of the fall. They saw it all. Took pity on a broken orphan boy.

Did they treat you well?

They weren't blood. They weren't you.

I'm not your blood.

You're the closest thing. You should have come to find me.

Are you going to drag me back down to the valley to punish me?

Maybe I am. You can take your chances and swing down now. But I'd advise against it. There's a pack of men after you as wild as dogs. And they don't even care about you enough to punish you.

Seems I'm done for either way.

Seems you are.

They rode along in silence and although Jessie looked out for him, there was never any sign of Jack Brown.

When they heard the sound of riders coming up the lower track both of them froze.

Fuck, said Barlow, *my badge. Where's my badge? Jessie, feel in the pack. Find my badge.*

She flipped up the leather top and searched through the pack.

There's handcuffs but no badge.

Put them around our ankles.

What?

Fucking do it.

Jessie secured their ankles together as four men rode around the bend.

What's this? said the one in the lead.

Look here. A boy and his pony and a suspicious-looking lady.

Would you call 'er that?

The four men rode in close.

She's the prize. You've got the prize.

Gentlemen, my name is Sergeant Andrew Barlow. His voice was wavering.

I wouldn't call 'er a lady and I wouldn't call us gentlemen, one of the men sniggered.

I'm a sergeant of the law and this woman is under arrest.

A sergeant?

Where's your badge?

It's in my pack.

The men started laughing until the one in the lead raised his gun and turned to him.

Sergeant, how about if you don't hand her over, we will blow your fucking head off.

It's all right, Barlow, said Jessie. *I'll go with them.*

There's no choice to be made here, said Barlow. *They cannot take you.*

The men began to argue among themselves. *What if he is the sergeant that he says he is? Should we kill him? We can't kill him. Let's kill him. There's no law in these mountains. A man can rape or kill and expect no consequence except his own consequence. You mean conscience? Consequence is what I said and what I mean to say!*

In their arguing, the men seemed to forget their purpose.

So what will it be? said Barlow.

The men all raised their guns and then one of them dismounted and stripped Jessie and Barlow of the guns they carried. *We'll ride till we find a camp and then we'll decide what to do with you. So just be good little soldiers now and follow our lead.*

Jessie and Barlow kept quiet, each wondering if the other was forging a plan. The men and the perilous slope of the mountain had finally hemmed them in and neither of them had any idea of how to escape.

When Jack Brown heard the rabble of voices, he stayed well back and hidden. He squatted in the bush and, listening, discerned that there were four men. He had no clarity other than that. He did not know what to do.

He knew he could not do nothing. If he acted now, what was the right way to act? There was no law to guide him except his instinct to protect Jessie and then the terrible feeling that until this moment, for all of his instinct, he had not protected her. So how could he trust himself now?

Jack Brown stalked them. He kept low in the bush and he knew if he had any powers to be invisible, now was the time to find them. He followed them all day and they set up camp and when a roo appeared near him he lay right down on the ground, because he guessed that soon they would spot the roo and start taking potshots in his direction.

When it was dark, he got close enough to the camp to hear them. The men had already turned themselves to celebrating and he could see Barlow and Jessie tied up on the ground.

So what's a thousand pounds divided by four?

Dunno.

You blockhead. It's two hundred and fifty, all divided.

They were sculling whiskey and they were staggering around the fire.

So do we get more for her alive or dead?

Doesn't matter. It's all the same. We're better to keep her alive than to have to drag her carcass down the mountain. If she's all rotted up, how can we prove it's her? Better to keep her in one piece.

The night passed more slowly than any night Jack Brown had ever known. The men were large and for all they drank they did not seem to relent from drinking more. Their talk was violent and Jack Brown felt sick with rage when one of them staggered over to where Jessie and Barlow were tied up and blindfolded them with his own stinking socks and began pissing on them.

But he must wait. He could not charge out and launch a show-down. The risk was of harming Jessie and the risk for him was too great. He must wait. It felt the same to him as when he had been fighting from the trenches. But even then the enemy did not seem so real as it did now.

He heard them: *So we can carve up the blondie and feed him to her. I've heard that eating human flesh will increase your sexual appetite. So we could be happy men and rich men, too.*

The men let out explosive laughs that Jack Brown thought would surely echo around the mountain. It was almost daylight again when they were finally asleep, though aside from their reclining bodies he could not be sure they were really sleeping.

He crept in anyway. Jessie and Barlow were lying twisted on the ground, still blindfolded. He did not disturb them.

He reached the closest man and with no hesitation cut his

throat. He kinked the man's neck so he would not gurgle and splutter and put his hand over his mouth in case he had any sound left in him. He moved from man to man in the same way and he was so silent about his task that none of the men woke the other and Jessie and Barlow did not hear him.

The last man opened his eyes as Jack Brown pulled the knife across his throat. He held his hand across the man's mouth and nose as the man struggled, the whites of his eyes turning over like stones in his head.

He cleaned the knife on the last man's coat and went to Jessie and Barlow and cut the ropes that bound them. They both stood up and fell over again, forgetting the cuffs that were still around their ankles.

Where's the key? whispered Jack Brown.

It's in my saddlebag.

Jack Brown sought out Barlow's horse from the others and unhooked the bag from the saddle. He emptied the bag on the ground and, finding the key to be there along with the police badge, threw them both to Barlow.

What are you doing? said the sergeant. *You'll wake them.*

They can't be woken, said Jack Brown.

Jack Brown led out three horses and Barlow's was one of them. They mounted the horses in silence. As Jack Brown set himself into the saddle he was aware that the last man who had sat in the saddle was now dead, and he was the man who had killed him.

VII

I have heard hard-hooved creatures moving over me, coming to drink at the river. I have heard dry trees falling down, split to their roots, and strong winds collecting topsoil as dry as dust. And through my stone pillow, I heard my mother.

They rode down into the valley, all three of them uneasy, two of them on stolen horses, Jessie in the middle, Jack Brown and Barlow on either side.

Each of them was a wreck, thin and hollow cheeked and looking grave. Both Jack Brown and Barlow had grown beards that were caked up with dust and the clothes on their backs were putrid and drenched with the sweat of fear. In an attempt to conceal herself, Jessie was wearing Jack Brown's hat, her hair tucked up inside it, and she wore Barlow's jacket to give her bulk that she did not have. As they rode, they hoped they looked like any three ragged men crossing the field.

It's not safe to go back to the hut, said Barlow. *We'll take you to the Seven Sisters. You'll be safer there till the constabulary arrive tomorrow.*

You mean safe till I'm arrested?

You're still worth a thousand pounds to any man who can read a poster or hear a rumor. So take your punt.

Who has that kind of money anyway? asked Jessie.

It's probably all a ruse, said Jack Brown. *But there's enough men now who believe it.*

They were quiet for a while and then Jessie said, *Sergeant, why are we crossing here in broad daylight?*

Because there's nowhere to hide. Barlow was rigid in the saddle, kept his eyes straight ahead.

They all breathed shallowly with the suspense of knowing they could be killed by a distant shot at any moment.

They rode on.

The wind picked up and Jessie had to hold down the hat on her head. They kicked their horses to a gallop and swayed out so they rode with the wind at their backs. They kept pace with one another and found a rhythm as they rode through the long and crackling grass, and under the midday sun shimmering waves of heat rose up from the open field and from the far view made their separate forms indistinct from one another.

When they reached the gate of the Seven Sisters it was almost dark. Jessie had never been inside the Seven Sisters though she had often ridden past it, wondering if Fitz was in there. She noticed that it now looked like a welcoming homestead, which was different from any other time she had seen it.

Barlow pulled up his horse at the gate and was staring at the sky.

What are you waiting for? said Jack Brown. *I thought you had enough stargazing in the mountains.*

I'm not coming with you. I need to get to the postmaster's hut and send a message to get the constabulary here by tomorrow, to get her out alive. Barlow handed Jack Brown the handcuffs. *They'll need to see* these on her and for God's sake make sure she's not armed because they won't have any compunction in shooting her.

Is there another option? said Jack Brown.

Barlow shifted in his saddle. *The three of us could keep riding till we get shot*, said Barlow.

I'm a very dangerous woman to ride with, said Jessie. She laughed but behind it was the tired hollowness of it all.

It's time, said Barlow. He turned his horse away from the gate and set off in the direction of the postmaster's hut.

Bandy! Jessie yelled. *Your jacket.*

Keep it, he yelled back. *There's a present for you in the pocket.*

Jack Brown kicked his horse and headed up the track but Jessie did not move. She sat on her horse and watched Barlow drift into the night.

arlow rode into the darkness. He knew himself changed. He could make sense of the place better in the dark, in a way he could not comprehend it through the heat and the glaring sun. The valley softened as the night sky opened up, and he knew where he was. He could feel but not see the mountains in the distance, the fields, the forest, the river, and it felt as true as any dream he had dreamt and he was relieved that the dream would soon be over.

Barlow knocked on the door of the postmaster's hut and found the man awake and inside. The postmaster was already tapping messages.

I've a message that's more urgent than the rest.

What is that, Sergeant?

Barlow sat down beside the man at his desk and wrote out the words on a piece of paper: CONSTABULARY NEEDED NOW. SEVEN SISTERS. LADY BUSHRANGER CAUGHT. ANARCHY ON THE MOUN-TAINS.

You got her? said the postmaster.

Barlow did not reply.

Are you ready to be a hero, Sergeant?

I think it is too late for that, said Barlow.

BARLOW RODE UNDER THE STARS as a man unafraid of death. Riding up Old Road, he felt, at last, like he was a light himself.

When he entered the hut, he did not bother to spark up a lantern. He could see well enough that the place had been trashed. He knew where there was rope and he was grateful that the rope alone had not been disturbed.

He walked out to the tree in front of the hut and threw the rope around its thickest branch. And then, holding tight to the rope, he climbed up the trunk of the tree. He perched in the V of the branch and tied the rope around his ankles. Then he threw himself back. The loops in the rope tightened around his legs and spun him, around and around, beneath the tree.

He was conscious enough to reflect that if he had hung himself by his neck his death would have surely come faster. But this was the way he chose, to give himself slowly over to gravity, vertebra by vertebra. It was his own death and he did not fear it.

J ack Brown and Jessie rode up the widening track to the house. When they reached the back entrance, Jack Brown swung down from his horse. The kitchen door was open and the madam burst out.

Jack! We've missed you! When are you going to give up your post at the policeman's hut and come join us here for good?

Jack Brown walked towards the madam.

Hold up, she said. *Don't come any closer. You smell like a fucking trooper yourself. You need a wash and a good feed. And by the looks of her, so does your friend.*

What I need is a favor, said Jack Brown. *I need a safe place to hide Jessie for the night. There's a few rough men out to get her.*

And us all! The madam laughed. *She'll be right as rain. Is Lay Ping expecting you tonight?*

No.

She'll be real glad you're here, Jack Brown. You're all that we hear about these days.

The madam set Jessie up in a room and gave her a silk robe for the evening and a skirt and a cotton blouse to change into in the morning. Jessie washed herself in the basin and put on the robe, which felt like cold water against her skin. She lay back on the four-poster bed with its flounces and embroidered flowers. A room like this was so foreign to her.

That night she did not sleep. She stared up at the canopy of the bed. With candles burning on wooden chests on each side of it, the room cast its own moving shadows upon the canopy. She saw there a boy on a trapeze, his shadow moving along the roof of a circus tent. And just as she had seen happen so many years before, there he was, stepping out across the rope and falling.

When she closed her eyes she saw herself hovering over the place where he landed. She could see her own hands stroking the dust where his limbs had fanned out, where his fingers had made trails.

When the constabulary arrived the next day, Jessie was sitting on the veranda of the homestead, her feet cuffed together. She was wearing a style of dress she had never worn. The cotton blouse the madam had given her had a ruffle on each shoulder and the skirt fanned out in pleats. Before the sun was up, she had dressed and combed out her hair from its tangle of knots. All kinds of leaf matter had rained around her, and it was the only thing left of her in the Seven Sisters because she had fed her own clothes to the fire.

Jack Brown sat beside her.

They sat in silence and watched the six members of the constabulary beating a track towards them, tall in their saddles with a spare horse between them.

Fuck, Jessie, said Jack Brown. *Why didn't you escape?*

I'm not dead yet, Jack Brown, she said and there was a grin on her face that Jack Brown had not seen for a very long time.

Thanks for the hat, she said. *Does it suit me?*

It's dangerous out there now, Jessie. Everybody wants a piece of you.

When the officers arrived they did not regard Jack Brown. They just lined themselves up in front of my mother and one of them said, *Are you Jessie Henry?*

Call me Jessie Bell or Jessie Hunt or Jessie Payne, but not Jessie Henry, that was never really my name.

It's all over now, Jessie.

Two of the younger officers made a seat for her by crossing their arms and she held on to their shoulders as they carried her to her horse.

This is the special treatment, she said. *Officers, this is surely the nicest arrest I've ever had.*

The horse they had brought for her to ride was fitted with a sidesaddle. It was awkward even to look at and, more than being arrested, it was the thing that angered her the most.

Jack Brown held on to the balustrade.

Jessie raised her hand to him and smiled and said, *Jack Brown.*

Jessie, he called after her.

She tipped her hat and said, *Jack Brown, long life.*

Jack Brown gave more of a salute than a wave and then he tucked his hand under his armpit and he was disturbed by the force of his heart and the rate it was beating. He watched the constabulary charge off, and Jessie, riding between them, her hair whipping out in all directions. There were two men in front of her, one on either side and two behind her, all holding guns. How could she possibly escape?

She did not turn around for a final glance or a wave, but Jack Brown kept his eyes fixed on the back of her and watched her figure shrinking in the distance. He had an impulse to run after her, to track her, to follow her. But he knew it was time to leave that impulse behind.

Standing there, he remembered his first sight of her, sitting by the river, contemplating what? He did not know. She looked to him now, as she had looked to him then, like a shifting thing on the landscape.

Soon she would be gone completely.

He wondered if she had always been an illusion and what, of any of it, had actually been real. Once upon a time, he had held her, he had smelt her, he had buried his own face in her hair. With his own ears he had worn her silence, her laughter, her swearing, and with his own eyes he had seen her spit and ride and fall. She was real. He had prints and tracks and memories to prove it.

Fuck, Jessie, he said and a tear rolled down his face and he knew then the truth of it. She would never be what he wanted her to be for him. She was not his lover and she was not his wife and she would never be. All his dreams of the two of them riding off together like two elemental forces combined, the mystery of what they might do together if they actually chose each other, all of that folded in beside him, an untracked path.

Jack Brown did not hear Lay Ping opening the door or walking across the veranda to stand beside him. But he did feel her hand upon his back and from just the warmth of it, he thought he might dissolve.

Come, she said finally. *Come and lay down with me.*

It was still early morning and no one was about, and they entered the house as if the house were their own. He followed Lay Ping, followed the tail of her robe, the swing of her hips, the twists of her hair. And in her room he followed her lead and they undressed and stood in front of each other. Then he was aware that everything in the room was utterly still except for their bodies, which were quivering.

Jack Brown took hold of her hips and he kissed her shoulder and with his mouth he followed the trail of her tattoo down to the dip of her back. Then he knelt behind her; looking up, the view was as supple and miraculous as a mountain. Scattered above her arse were the tattoos of rocks, the god and a goddess and the word SORROW. Kneeling there, holding on to the bones of her hips, Jack Brown was grateful that he was a man and not a myth and that he was alive enough to feel the heat of the body in front of him.

The constabulary rode all day and they camped at night with my mother between them. The next morning they were up at first light as the fields folded around them, and they stopped only when one of the officers dropped his gun.

My mother was not lying then when she said, *I've an awful pain in my gut, Sergeant.*

Keep riding, men, yelled back the lead sergeant.

If I could just relieve myself, she pleaded.

The lead sergeant kicked his horse.

Sergeant, I'd hate for there to be an accident on your lovely saddle and your lovely pony.

All right, stop! said the sergeant. *Let the convict down.*

But her feet are cuffed, said one of the officers. *And she says she needs to relieve herself.*

She'll have to find some way, said the sergeant.

The two young officers helped her down.

Conceal yourself behind that tree, said the sergeant, pointing to the near distance. *We don't need to see you or any woman disgracing herself. But you must yell and you must keep on yelling.*

I'm sorry, Sergeant, said my mother. *This may take a while.*

Be quick, woman, and get it over and done with and do not waste our time.

The police officers watched her as she jumped, her legs cuffed together, jumping all the way to the tree.

I'm here, she yelled.

That's it. Keep on yelling, said the sergeant.

Behind the tree my mother yelled, *I'm here*, as she plunged a hand into the neck of her blouse and pulled out the key she had found in Barlow's jacket. She opened the locks of the cuffs around her ankles easily and quietly, all the time yelling, *I'm here*. She yelled as she slipped off her skirt and dropped to the ground and she yelled as she dug her elbows into the dirt.

Then my mother scuttled out into the long grass, as any escaping creature would do, except she had a clear voice within her and she yelled, *I'm here, I'm here*. And then she was silent.

In the valley, sound travels and distance is difficult to judge. Voices echo and you may never find their true source.

When they did not hear her, the officers stepped tentatively towards the tree.

Jessie! they cried. *Jessie, are you there?*

But she was not. Only the cuffs were on the ground with the madam's skirt.

The officers mounted their horses again and sought her in different directions. But north, south, east and west, they did not find her.

She was on her stomach, snaking through the long, dry grass.

JESSIE IS *MY* MOTHER.

Forward and back I have tracked her. I have heard her like a song. I caught her voice here and there, and when I finally pieced it together, distinguished it all from the din, I knew she was mine to hear. I tracked her and all that she loved and some she did not, to *know* my mother. And then, as I felt in my own heart a wish for her freedom, in one single and shimmering note I heard her. She said: *I am here*.

THE STORY BEHIND THE STORY

As a teenager growing up in Australia in the Hunter Valley, about one hundred fifty miles north and inland from Sydney, I heard about a wild woman who hid out in a mountain cave not far from where I lived.

There was nothing written down about her life then. I didn't even know her name. And what I did know was all hearsay: she was a trick rider, horse rustler, wanted woman. Her story seemed to be made of air more than earth, like a fairy tale, and just like that it took hold of my imagination.

Apparently she had lived and roamed in the area in the early 1920s, but it felt truer to me that she was still out there in the mountains sleeping rough, eating weeds and scraping through the bush.

I thought about her every day.

Just as soon as I was old enough, I left the Hunter Valley and I forgot about her. I filled my mind with more immediate things—adventure, study, love. And each had a way of covering up her story. I came to it again only through dissatisfaction in what I was reading and seeing. I knew plenty of unlikely heroines in life, but they seemed to be missing from history and fiction.

In my twenties, I started teaching creative writing for a living. I often launched the workshops with an appeal to students to "tell the story you most need to tell." Of course, this is easy enough to say but much less easy to do.

Around this time, along with another writer, I was invited to travel to isolated country areas, including the Hunter Valley, to run a series of writing workshops. It was a wonderful gig. Mostly, I saw it as a chance to be paid well and escape the bustle of Sydney. I had no inkling of how the trip would shape me.

We drove happily down into the Hunter Valley and then out along the dusty roads to the Widden Valley. In each place we felt the fullness of local hospitality. One of the venues was an old timber hall in the middle of a paddock with the mountain ranges in view. For generations the hall had been the community meeting place for weddings, wakes and christenings. You could actually see dance steps worn into the floor.

After I had spent two days there, working with students of all stripes and ages—an equine dentist, a mother, the mayor—one woman gave me the gift of a book. It was an amateur historian's account of that wild woman who had lived in the mountain cave. But now she had a name. She was Jessie Hickman.

I drove back to Sydney with the queasiest feeling. In part, it was the strangeness of having forgotten about her, like forgetting a dear friend. And then this new and sudden sense of responsibility towards her or, more accurately, to her story. I hadn't even reached the highway and already there was a strong argument forming in my head. This woman had a name, a birthplace. She was fact and I wrote fiction.

This argument continued for the four-hour drive back to Sydney and then went on for the next five years or so. Fact versus fiction. Even so, Jessie Hickman inspired enough daring in me to surreptitiously seek out prison records and social histories, all in the hope of finding more traces.

After years of her fantastical presence in my life, when I found Jessie's prison mug shot, she became solid to me. There she was: "Jessie McIntyre alias Bell alias Payne" (not yet known as Hickman), "of eyes brown," "of hair dark brown," "special features: nil." For me, her smudged eyes were the missing piece. Coal-dark, they were earth itself, expressing everything that took me a whole novel to say.

I copied this image of Jessie, took it home, framed it. I hung it above my desk—which, in hindsight, was a foolish thing to do. Her face is so intimidating. The way her jaw juts out challenges all that might be false or whimsical. I was stuttering beneath it. I wanted to get her story right, to give her a voice, to tell her story from her point of view. But what I was learning of her, no question, was that here was a woman of action, not words.

Since the book's publication, some readers have asked me, "Why choose to tell the story through the dead and buried baby?"

The simplest answer is, I couldn't tell Jessie's story any other way.

For me, the child as narrator is that part of Jessie she had to bury because of the plain brutality of her life. Her softness had no place in the rough world where she found herself. So more than anything, that is what I wanted to give voice to, that is the story I needed to tell.

Recently, I went back to the Hunter Valley on a book tour. While I was there, I met an older woman who asked me how I knew that Jessie had given birth to a premature child who did not survive. I told her I didn't know for sure, there was no record of it. Then I added, a little defensively, "Well, it is fiction, after all."

The woman had no interest in my fact-versus-fiction debate. She began telling me her own story—how she'd lived her whole life at the foothills of the Widden Valley ranges where Jessie had roamed, how her father used to take her on long drives looking for lost sheep and cattle. One day he pulled up on the side of the road near a river and said, "This is where Jessie Hickman lost her child."

I don't know if the woman's story is true. There is no way to know. It is hearsay, after all. And people do like to tell stories. But what I have learned, or rather, grown into, is a faith in fiction. Because no matter how far you take it, fiction always circles back. Somehow it always wants to tell the truth.

—*Courtney Collins*

ACKNOWLEDGMENTS

For THEIR UNIQUE PART in the life of this book (in chronological order), heartfelt thanks to my agents Benython Oldfield and Sharon Galant of Zeitgeist Media Group, Jane Palfreyman, Clara Finlay, Ali Lavau, Juliette Ponce, Erika Abrams, Sam Redman, Clare Drysdale, Stéphanie Abou, Amy Einhorn, Liz Stein, Inés Planells, Silvia Querini, Ageeth Heising, Marianne Schönbach, Ilse Delaere, Maaike le Noble and Norbert Uzseka.

For their care and support, special thanks to Caroline Baum, Daniel Campbell, Kirsty Campbell, Siobhán Cantrill, Louise Cornegé, Alison Drinkwater, Angie Hart, Anna Helm, Fiona Kitchin, Lilith Lane, Gareth Liddiard, Kathryn Liddiard, Lisa Madden, Jeanmarie Morosin, Kate Richardson, Jackie Ruddock, Amanda Roff, Jasmin Tarasin, Jo Taylor and Meredith Turnbull.

And to my family—Collins, Diffley and Field combined, thanks and love always.

Readers Guide

THE UNTOLD

DISCUSSION QUESTIONS

1. Who is the narrator of *The Untold*? Do you consider the narrator to be reliable, or unreliable? Is *The Untold* the narrator's experience of Jessie, or Jessie's life as seen (or not seen) by the narrator?

2. What is the author's purpose in beginning the narration with the question: "If the dirt could speak whose story would it tell"?

3. Consider the following quote: "That is all I know: death is a magic hall of mirrors and within it there is a door and the door opens both ways . . ." (p. 13). How does *The Untold* challenge the finite notion of death?

4. The author states that "This is Australia. The dirt is a morgue." What does *The Untold* say about colonial Australia?

5. What is the significance of Jack Brown's relationship with Lay Ping and The Seven Sisters?

6. Consider the motivation for Andrew Barlow's final actions. Why do you think he made the decision he did?

7. What do you think is the significance of Andrew Barlow asking Jack Brown, " . . . are you black enough to be my tracker?"? How does this relate to America's civil rights history?

8. How does the landscape reveal the characters? To what extent is it oppressive and to what extent is it redemptive?

9. Consider Jessie's role as an escape artist. In what ways does she reveal herself as one?

10. Discuss Andrew Barlow and Jessie's relationship. How does it connect with Jessie's relationship with the boy, Joe, Bill and the other riders in the gang?

11. Why do you think the author diverts the narrative in one section to a man who has been buried for forty years? What is his relationship to the other characters, in particular, the old woman and the old man who find Jessie by the river?

12. What do you make of the ending? What do you think it means, "And then, as I felt in my own heart a wish for her freedom, in one single and shimmering note I heard her. She said: I am here."?

ABOUT THE AUTHOR

COURTNEY COLLINS grew up in the Hunter Valley in New South Wales, Australia. She completed her first novel, *The Untold*, in an old postmaster's cottage on the Goulburn River in regional Victoria. She now lives in a seaside town in NSW and is working on her second novel, *The Walkman Mix*.

Visit the author online at courtneycollinswriter.com, facebook.com/CourtneyCollins/Author, or twitter.com/cc_author.